The Wonderful Wishes of B.

Also by Katherin Nolte

Back to the Bright Before

The Wonderful Wishes of B.

Katherin Nolte

RANDOM HOUSE 🏠 NEW YORK

Text copyright © 2024 by Katherin Nolte
Jacket art copyright © 2024 by Jen Bricking
Jacket lettering copyright © 2024 by Sarah Coleman

Visit us on the Web! rhcbooks.com

Educators and librarians, for a variety of teaching tools, visit us at RHTeachersLibrarians.com

Library of Congress Cataloging-in-Publication Data is available upon request.
ISBN 978-0-593-56514-8 (trade) — ISBN 978-0-593-56515-5 (lib. bdg.) — ISBN 978-0-593-56516-2 (ebook)

The text of this book is set in 11.5-point Berling LT Std.
Interior design by Michelle Crowe
Cat illustrations by Michelle Crowe
Postcard art by MicroOne and folded paper art by Sharpshot used under license from stock.adobe.com

Printed in the United States of America
10 9 8 7 6 5 4 3 2 1
First Edition

For my own Glad: I miss you.

Chapter 1

I t all started with Neptune. Not the planet. The cat. Though he wasn't named Neptune yet. He was just an anonymous kitten stuck in a waterspout, and I was trying to save him. That's what I told him, too.

"Please stop scratching me," I said. "I'm trying to save your life."

It was New Year's Day. Glad was dead and always would be. That was the truth and a point-blank fact.

Here's another fact: there are many ways to miss somebody.

You can miss what they looked like, or how they smelled, or the feel of their palm in your hand. You can miss the sound of their voice or the space their life took up in your head. You can miss the notes they left, tucked in your lunch box or slipped in your sock drawer or hidden in the pages of your books.

I missed my grandma Glad all the ways. Every single one of them: all the ways I could think of, and all the ways I couldn't think of, too.

But back to the kitten.

When I told him I was trying to save his life, either the cat thought I was lying or he didn't understand. Because he started to scratch me even more, like he was pretending my arm was a scratch-and-sniff sticker, and he wanted to get all the smell out.

What the Cat-Who-Would-Be-Named-Neptune didn't know, though, was that I was pretending, too. I was pretending his claws weren't bringing tears to my eyes, that I couldn't feel the beads of blood sprouting on my wrist.

What Future Planet couldn't see was that the whole experience—me crouched on the sidewalk in my polka-dot pajamas and fuzzy slippers, arm jammed inside a waterspout—was a good one. It was training for my goal. Which was this:

I wanted to stop feeling.

You know the Tin Man, who wanted a real, beating heart? Well, I was a real, beating girl who wanted to be a Tin Man. Right in the center of my chest is where I wanted to be him, to replace the horrible muscle that pumped and pumped, filling my life with feelings.

I was sick of missing Glad, sick of all my other feelings, too. So I'd decided to do something about it.

See, what I imagined was my heart, all stretched out and bumpy. The bumps were my feelings. Every time I didn't cry or wince or think, *I wish I could see her again*, it was like I was taking a mallet and hitting one of those bumps. The more times I hit, the smoother my heart got, till one day, it wouldn't be muscle anymore, but perfectly flat, like a sheet of metal. Goodbye, heart. Hello, Tin Man.

I got down on my stomach and pressed my face to the waterspout. Two eyes shone back.

"You think you're hurting me," I told the eyes, "but really you're helping me. The more you scratch, the less I feel. The less I feel, the more metallic I become."

The kitten hissed.

"I've got all day," I told him. "I have absolutely nowhere to go."

"Who you talkin' to?" a voice asked.

Unfortunately, the voice did not belong to the kitten.

I stayed on my stomach, eye pressed to the metal

spout. The voice belonged to a boy. *Maybe*, I thought, *if I lie here and don't say anything, the voice will go away.* I decided to count to twenty in my head. *One . . . two . . .*

"Why aren't you answerin' me?" the voice asked.

Three . . . four . . .

"Can't you hear?"

The voice was kind of rude. *Five . . . six . . .*

"What you lookin' at?"

Seven . . .

"Can I see it?"

It was also rather annoying. *Eight . . . nine . . .*

"You might cut yourself. That metal looks sharp."

Ten . . .

"Rusty, too. I bet you'll get tetanus."

The voice was a bit of a worrywart. *Eleven . . . twelve . . .*

"Your whole face will fall off. Green slime'll leak from your eyes."

The voice didn't know much about infections. *Thirteen . . . fourteen . . .*

"Well, I tried bein' nice to you. I guess I'll have to be mean instead."

Fifteen . . . sixteen . . .

"I'm gonna kick you."

The voice was violent. *Seventeen . . .*

"As hard as I can. And that's really hard because I'm superstrong."

The voice was *very* violent. *Eighteen* . . .

"I'm the strongest kid in Ohio. Plus, I got steel-toed boots—with nails stickin' out the ends."

Hmm . . . The voice was probably lying. *Nineteen* . . .

"Okay. You're gonna regret this. Here I go—"

"Don't." I sat up.

The voice was, indeed, a liar. The boy was not wearing steel-toed boots with nails sticking out at the ends. In fact, he wasn't wearing boots at all. He had on a pair of dirty sneakers with a hole in both toes. I could see his socks.

"You're a liar," I told him.

The boy shrugged. "My name's Caleb Chernavachin," he said, as if that explained everything, as if a boy named Caleb Chernavachin could not help but be a liar.

I stared at him. His face was round and covered in freckles, like someone had taken a saltshaker full of freckles and shaken them all over his head. He had short, straw-colored hair with long bangs that stuck straight up off his forehead. He wore a puffy winter coat that was so small he couldn't zip it, and the sleeves came up to his elbows. He was a ridiculous-looking boy. I wanted nothing to do with him.

"What's your name?" he asked.

"Beatrice Corwell."

"Are you ten?"

I nodded.

"So am I," he said, and tilted back on his heels as if that were really something.

"There are a lot of people in the world who are ten," I told him. "So, really, we have nothing in common."

"Yeah, well, my dad is a famous wrestler. So I'm richer than you are."

"I'm not rich at all." I lay down again on the sidewalk with my face to the waterspout. "I'm going to get back to saving you as soon as this boy leaves," I whispered in case the kitten thought I'd forgotten.

Neptune-to-Be hissed.

"Who you talkin' to?" Caleb asked.

"No one." I sat up again.

"Why aren't you wearin' a coat?"

"It's bad luck to wear a coat on New Year's Day." I don't know why I said that. I didn't believe it; I just made it up on the spot. That happened to me a lot. I'd open my mouth, and out would spill words I hadn't planned to say. It was, my teacher said, *a fatal flaw.*

The real reason I didn't have on a coat was because I'd forgotten to put one on when I ran outside.

I'd been sitting in Glad's room, staring at Bright Baby, when I heard the kitten. Despite being on the second floor, I could hear its cry plain as day. (I was a natural-born cat rescuer, which was why I already had seven of them.) So I flew down the staircase—even though it was January and cold as a Popsicle, even though I had on polka-dot pajamas and fuzzy slippers.

Caleb Chernavachin looked at those slippers and said, "You sure are dressed funny."

I stared at his too-small coat. "Have you looked in the mirror?"

"Your hair, too. It's all crooked or somethin'."

Now, that was the truth and a point-blank fact. My hair was the color of mud, cut just below my chin, and very crooked. That was because my mom had cut it, and she was a horrible haircutter. When Glad was alive, my hair had been a thing of great beauty. I looked like one of the models whose pictures hang in beauty salons. In fact, I *was* a haircut model whose headshot hung in Glad's beauty parlor. It still hung there, actually. But now, thanks to my mom, I no longer looked anything like my picture.

I didn't tell this to Caleb, though. I just said, "Your bangs stick straight up in the air like porcupine quills."

Caleb touched his quills with his palm. "I'm very rich."

I eyed his big toes. "I've never met a rich person with such holey shoes."

"It's the new style," he said, then changed the subject. "I saw you at school. Did you see me?"

I shrugged. *Maybe yes, maybe no* is what my shoulders said. But the real answer was yes, I'd seen him. It was impossible not to. Mrs. Hartley had stood in front of the room two weeks ago and said, "Class, we have a new student. His name is—"

But I had stopped listening. Porcupine-headed boys didn't interest me. It was the last day of school before Christmas vacation, and I was thinking about my cats. All seven of them. I'd needed to make them presents.

"You want me to help you get that cat outta there?" the ridiculous boy asked.

"How'd you know it was a cat?"

He grinned. "I'm smart. I got ESP. Plus, I can see through walls."

You can tell why I called him ridiculous. "No thanks."

Caleb shrugged. "Your loss, Beatrice. Happy New Year." He walked on down the sidewalk.

"New Year," I called to his back. I did not say *happy*. No year without Glad in it could be happy.

I turned to the waterspout. "Okay. I'm done messing around. It's time to be saved." I got on my stomach and took a deep breath and closed my eyes. Then I thrust my arm into the metal tube and wrapped my fingers around a furry body.

The kitten screamed. He clawed. He cried. Then he was out in the open, and I was seeing him for the first time.

He was puffy and black with robin's-egg eyes. He was the cutest thing that had ever existed. My heart swelled up super fat.

Which was a problem.

Tin Men don't love kittens. But—I wasn't a Tin Man yet. My heart was a work in progress.

"You shall be called Neptune," I told the kitten, who flailed about, trying to escape my grasp. I cupped him close to my chest and pressed my mouth to the top of his dusty head.

The kitten settled down then. They always do.

"I'll take you home, and my mom will give you a bath." Even though my mom was horrible at cutting human hair, she was very good at styling cats.

I looked around the downtown, which was empty.

Seven o'clock in the morning on New Year's Day, and no one was out except me, and Neptune, and Caleb Chernavachin (wherever he was).

And even though this new year was going to be horrible, and even though I was so cold I felt part snowman—I smiled because of the kitten. But I did not feel happy. Tin Men never feel happy.

I walked down the sidewalk to my grandma Glad's beauty parlor. GLAD'S, read the big purple letters on the building. The parlor was empty and dark. If Glad were a ghost, I might have seen her in there. But Glad wasn't a ghost. Glad was far away, in heaven, a place that couldn't be seen with human eyes.

I climbed the metal steps, to the upstairs apartment. I imagined hot cocoa for me and a saucer of milk for Neptune. But before I opened the door, I paused.

I'd just thought of something.

Life happens in threes. First, one toy breaks, then another, and another. If a kid's rude to you in math class, you know you'll get it in English and social studies, too.

Well, I'd just met two somebodies: one in a waterspout, one in an itty-bitty coat. That meant there was one more somebody to go.

Standing on the stairs, I looked down at the town.

Buildings dark, traffic circle empty—not a soul in sight. But someone was out there. Someone extra-ordinary, with the power to change everything.

And I knew that someone was just waiting for the right moment to arrive.

Chapter 2

I know a lot. Not as much as my best friend, Dianne of the Flame-Red Hair, of course. She knows everything. That's because she lives out in the country—at least she used to, before she moved to Florida. She lived in a little house with an herb garden in the back. She'd pick spearmint leaves, and we'd chew them like gum. We'd gather wild strawberries, and Dianne knew how to smash them and mix them with sugar and turn them into jam. A creek ran through the middle of her yard, and we'd spend all day looking for fossils. Dianne knew all about fossils, especially trilobites. Her dream was to find a trilobite and put it on display in her bedroom.

Dianne was tough, too. She'd climb apple trees so high that her knees got scraped bloody, but she never winced. In public, she was kind of solemn, but that's only because she had so many thoughts colliding in her head. When we were alone, she'd flash a secret smile so bright it made me squint. What I'm trying to say is, not only is Dianne of the Flame-Red Hair the toughest, most interesting girl in the world, she's also a genius.

And I'm pretty smart, too.

That's not bragging. It's just the truth and a point-blank fact. Glad is who made me so smart. When she was dying in her bed, I sat beside her and held her bony hand.

It took Glad a long time to die. Weeks and weeks. The days piled up like bones. I'd talk to her, but she couldn't talk back. She just lay there, eyes closed, long gray hair spread out like a fan. You can only talk so much till your voice starts to hurt. So I'd stop, and then I'd get bored. That's why I started reading the encyclopedia.

Glad had a whole set—twenty-six books in all. I started at *Aachen* and read all the way to *Zworykin*. Twenty-six books. That's how long it took Glad to die. And that's why I know so much.

Like about wishes, how heavy they are. And how, when you have too many of them, they start to weigh you down, like books in your backpack. I'd look out my apartment window and count wishes on my fingers.

I wish Glad hadn't died.
I wish Dianne hadn't moved to Florida.
I wish my mom could cut hair.
I wish my dad would come back.

Plus, one more wish that was tip-top secret and hurt, like a hangnail, whenever I counted it.

Tin Men don't count wishes; I knew that. They don't stare out windows and touch their fingers. Tin Men look straight ahead, not thinking about what could be or has been. They only think about what *is*.

But enough about wishes.

Now that I'd saved Neptune, I had to introduce him to his brothers.

The apartment above Glad's beauty parlor was small: wood floors, flat ceilings, and two bedrooms. Glad had had her own bedroom, and the cats and I shared a room, which left my mom to sleep on the futon in the living room.

I took Neptune to my room and closed the door. Then I set him on the middle of my solar system bedspread. "Boys," I called, "come meet your new brother."

Slowly, one by one, from behind desks and under box springs and inside curtains, the seven brothers appeared.

There was Mercury, a sandy Maine coon; Venus, the curly-haired Cornish Rex; Earth, a blue-gray domestic shorthair; Mars, a red Persian; Jupiter, the spotted fatty; Saturn, a wild-eyed tabby; and Uranus, the long-haired white runt. They jumped onto my bed and formed a circle around Neptune.

That's when my mom poked her head in.

"What are you doing, Beatrice?" She had on her gold headband, her big silver glasses, and her red lipstick.

"I'm trying to complete the solar system."

She looked at Neptune. "Is that another cat?"

"He's the last planet."

"I thought Uranus was the last planet."

"No, Mom. There are *eight* planets. Uranus is only number seven."

"Fine. But he's the last one. Even if they discover more planets. No more cats—okay?" My mom ended most of her sentences with that word: *okay*. Even though she was not okay. She was *overwhelmed*. That's what I heard her whisper on the phone when she thought I wasn't listening.

"Okay," I said, because I wanted her to leave so I could get back to my introductions.

But instead of leaving, she said, "I've got to do some bookkeeping downstairs. Will you be fine up here?" My mom was good at bookkeeping—unlike cutting hair. She'd always been the beauty parlor's accountant. It was only after Glad got sick that she had to be the haircutter, too.

"Of course," I said.

"I'll help you bathe that little guy later, okay? Love you."

"Love you," I said, and then she left. I turned to the cats. "Where were we?"

"Meow," said Mercury. He was the oldest and also the most helpful.

"That's right. Thank you." I stroked the top of his head. "I'd like to introduce you to your new brother, Neptune. Please welcome him into the family."

The cats swished their tails amicably—all except Uranus, who was jealous he was no longer the baby. He lifted a paw, as if to bop Neptune on the head. "No," I said in my you-are-a-very-bad-cat voice.

He lowered his paw.

"Since it's a special day," I continued, "you may all wear your bows." I took their bow tie collars out of my dresser and attached them to their necks. There was one for each color of the rainbow, starting with red for Mercury, all the way down to violet for Uranus. And I just happened to have a white bow tie for Neptune, which contrasted so adorably with his black fur that I had to scoop him up against my chest.

"Come along, the rest of you." I led them out of my room and into Glad's.

If there ever was a time to be a Tin Man, it was inside Glad's room. She had died in September, a month after Dianne of the Flame-Red Hair had moved away, but her room was still exactly as it had been. There was her bed, her desk, the bookshelf with the encyclopedia set. Stepping through her door was like entering a portal to the past. The only difference was, instead of Glad lying in the middle of the bed, there was a doll she'd owned when she was little.

The cats jumped onto the yellow comforter, and I set Neptune on the middle of the mattress. Then I pulled the desk chair over and took a seat. I looked at the doll but didn't pick her up. I never picked her up, because she wasn't mine; she belonged to Glad.

The doll was about a foot long, with a porcelain face and a swirl of painted blond hair. Her cheeks were pink, her lips the color of a strawberry. She had open-and-shut eyes and wore a white lace dress with a pocket on the chest. She was the prettiest doll in the world. That's the truth and a point-blank fact.

I had a name for her: Bright Baby.

I also had a wish for her, the fifth wish, the one that went on my pinkie when I counted the wishes on my fingers. The one that hurt and was tip-top secret. The wish was this: I wished Bright Baby would come to life and be my sister. I wished I could feed her a bottle, and rock her to sleep, and tuck her into a crib. I wished I could give her a bath, and brush her hair, and teach her all the things I'd learned in the encyclopedia set.

The truth was: life was lonely without Glad. The apartment was empty without her hidden notes to find. Life was gray, instead of in color. But if I had a sister, I wouldn't mind so much. If we were playing hide-and-seek or making pillow forts, the rooms wouldn't feel so bare and drab. What I'm trying to say is, a person can face just about anything with a sister at her side.

"Well, Bright Baby," I said, because that's what I did. Even though she was a doll, I talked to her.

Glad used to come every night, sit on my bed, and talk until I sank deep into dreamland. When she got sick, I went to her and let my words fill the air. Now there was just Bright Baby to tell my stories to. My mom was too *overwhelmed* to listen.

"Everyone keeps telling me Happy New Year," I continued, "but this year will not be happy or new—unless you come to life. That's Neptune there beside you. I rescued him this morning. Caleb Chernavachin wanted to help me. You should have seen his coat."

Bright Baby's eyes were closed, her head perfectly centered on Glad's pillow. The room was so quiet I could hear the clock tick.

"I've got five wishes," I said. "That's enough for a whole hand."

Then I almost started crying. I didn't mean to. I didn't *want* to. I knew it was against the Tin Man rules. But sometimes you can't control your tears. They just end up sneaking right out of you, like how you don't choose to release your breaths.

The cats watched me. They hated when I cried.

"I'm sorry to be like this," I said, clenching my eyes so the tears couldn't escape. "I'm trying, Bright Baby, to make my heart so hard."

Venus jumped off the bed.

I used my pajama sleeve to wipe my runny nose. "Where are you going?" I asked.

He leapt onto the desk. Then he perched on the edge, looked me right in the eye, and said, "Meow."

"I don't know what you're talking about."

He lifted his paw in Bright Baby's direction.

"You want me to do something with Bright Baby?"
He winked.

Usually, I don't let my cats boss me around, but there was something strange that day in the Unhappy Old Year air. Something crackly, like static. Every time I took a breath, my lungs quivered. Also, Venus was the steadiest of the felines; he wasn't one to make unreasonable demands.

So I stood up and put a hand on Bright Baby's lace dress. "Like this?"

Venus swished his curly-haired tail, jumped off the desk, and took his place back with his brothers on Glad's bed.

Then they waited. The clock ticked.

I thought about Glad. I thought of sitting in her beauty parlor as she curled my hair. I thought of what day it was—January 1—and how Glad and I always wrote New Year's resolutions, then taped them to the fridge.

I looked at the cats. "It's the resolutions, isn't it?"

One by one, they nodded their furry heads.

I closed my eyes, thinking. And then I remembered what Glad had always said: *The squeaky wheels get the grease.* What that means is, if you want something, you've got to ask for it. You can't just sit there and count it on your fingers. You've got to *act*. If you have a wish, you have to *make* it happen.

Well, I had five wishes, a whole hand. It was time to free up some fingers.

"This year, I resolve to make Bright Baby come to life," I said. And then I remembered another one of Glad's sayings: *Don't put all your eggs in one basket*, which is another way of saying, *Two New Year's resolutions are better than one.*

So I added, "I will also make Dianne of the Flame-Red Hair come back. There. How's that?"

Before the cats could reply, Bright Baby's eyes popped open—all on their own. There was something in the pocket of her dress!

I glanced at Venus, who nodded sagely. So I slipped two fingers into the pocket and pulled out a little piece of folded paper. Carefully, I unfolded it and knew immediately what it was.

A note from Glad.

Somehow, she'd left me a message, like she used to. Somehow, she'd gotten permission, in heaven, to tell me something, something important, something essential for me to know.

I read the note, then looked at the cats, at their sixteen curious eyes.

"This slip of paper is what's known as an *unexplained phenomenon*," I told them, which is a term I'd learned in the encyclopedia.

The cats stared at me, not understanding.

"Glad's leaving me notes again. She's got an important message, but because Bright Baby's pocket is so small, she's going to tell me one word at a time." I paused, nearly breathless. "Do you want to know the first word?"

They blinked in wild expectation.

"*DO*. The first word is *DO*. But DO *what*?" I asked.

The cats didn't know. Neither did I.

But that was okay; I was patient. I could wait for the next word. The main thing was, I had a note from Glad. Plus, I had my New Year's resolutions, which meant, pretty soon, I'd have two free fingers on my hand.

"Maybe this year won't be so bad after all," I told the boys, "*if* we take action."

So take action is exactly what we did.

Chapter 3

I kept something in my pocket, to help with the Tin Man Project. It was a leather cord with a string of beads. Every time I felt sad or angry, lonely or excited, I'd pull one of the beads. At the end of the day, I'd sit by Bright Baby and tell her how I fared.

"Five beads today," I'd say. Or, "Only three. Not bad."

Some days, though, were nothing but drama, and I'd pull my whole cord before noon. The goal was not to pull a single one. When that day arrived, my heart would be so flat you could poke my belly with a knife, and I wouldn't even blink.

Well, it was three days after the *unexplained phenomenon*, and I'd yet to pull a bead that morning. It was the last day before I'd have to go back to school, and I was walking across the town square. Glad's beauty parlor was on one corner, and there were all sorts of other shops around it. In the square's center was a traffic circle, and in the middle of that was a Christmas tree.

Glad used to hide a present for me under that tree every year. Christmas morning, she'd take me by the hand and lead me across the street, and there, at the base of that gigantic tree, would be a box with my name on it. This was the first year I hadn't stood with Glad under the enormous branches.

The cats were with me. I carried Neptune, but the others walked behind, in a straight line, wearing their bows because they liked to look fancy. We were headed to the courthouse fountain.

"We are problem solvers," I said to the cats. "We are beings of action!"

That's when Raejean stepped out of Cutie Pie Camera.

Oh great, I thought. *Just what I need when I'm trying to free up two fingers.* Then—because Tin Men don't have enemies; when they see an unpleasant person, they just *clink-clank* by, not a thought in their head—I had to pull a bead in my pocket.

"Hello, Beatrice," Raejean sang in the voice she used when she was trying to be annoying.

"Hello." I stopped a few feet from where she stood

by the door of her parents' shop. I looked at her—blond, curly hair, double-pierced ears, sparkly lip gloss—while she looked at my cats.

"You go everywhere with those things, don't you?"

"They're not *things*. And the answer is yes."

"Weird," she said.

"What's weird?"

"Oh, just that you'd rather hang out with cats than humans."

I'd known Raejean since kindergarten. We'd been enemies from the start, when we got in a fight over the plastic counting bears. "I've never liked the name Cutie Pie Camera," I told her.

Raejean put a hand on her hip. "It's better than GLAD'S."

My face flashed hot hate. I pulled a bead. "Don't you *ever* say bad things about my grandma."

"I'm talking about your *mom*, not your grandma. *My* mom says *your* mom is so bad at cutting hair that the only way she'd step foot in GLAD'S is if she was bald!"

"My mom wouldn't cut your mom's hair for a million dollars!"

"You *wish* you had a million dollars. My mom says GLAD'S is down to just one customer a day. She doesn't know how it's still in business."

"Your mom is a know-nothing nincompoop," I

yelled. Then I happened to glance at the boys, who were lined up on either side of me with worried looks. They hated when I lost my temper.

I pulled another bead.

"You're just jealous, Beatrice. You're jealous my mom has a successful business. Plus, you're jealous I have a dad."

"I have a dad," I said.

"Where is he?"

I thought for a moment, and then out popped the first place I could think of. "Antarctica."

Raejean fake-laughed. "Guess where my dad is. He's right in there." She pointed to the store window that had *Cutie Pie Camera* written in gold cursive letters on the glass.

I looked, even though I didn't want to. That's how Raejean's store was for me—I was drawn to it, despite hating it. I stared in its window, even though I wished the whole building would crumble to the ground.

Today, Raejean's dad was behind the counter while her mom held a camera and took pictures of a family posed in front of a brick-wall backdrop. The family was a mom, dad, boy, and girl, all with carrot-orange hair. The mom had her hands on the girl's shoulders. The dad had the boy on his back. They were smiling with their big white teeth.

And that's what I didn't like about Cutie Pie Camera—how everyone smiled and was so tooth-grinning happy. Like they couldn't even imagine what it was like to have a dead grandma, or a best friend who'd moved away, or a business nobody came to, or a dad who you didn't even know what continent he was on.

I looked at that other dad with the boy on his back. The dad leaned down, crossed his eyes at the girl, and stuck out his tongue, to make her laugh. I thought, *I'm sure happy I don't have a dad like that. I wouldn't take a dad like that if they were handing them out for free.*

I turned back to Raejean. "I've got a new kitten." I held up Neptune.

She squinted her eyes. "I'll show you something better."

She went into Cutie Pie Camera and came back with a pink leather purse. "This is Montgomery. He's a purebred Pomeranian. I got him for Christmas."

A fluffy puppy head poked from the purse. It had bulging eyes and a little pink tongue sticking out. It was the cutest thing I'd ever seen.

"I don't like dogs." I shrugged as if Montgomery was the most unsnuggable thing on the planet.

"Good. Then I won't let you pet him." Raejean

lifted the puppy out of the purse and held him in her palm.

My fingers trembled, longing to touch him, but I pulled a bead instead.

"Come on, boys," I told my cats. "Let's go work on those resolutions." The brothers obediently formed a line behind me. "Goodbye, Raejean-Is-Mean."

"Goodbye, Beatrice-Feet-Kiss."

And even though I wanted to say something so cruel that it would make Raejean weep, I didn't. I just walked away silently, like a Tin Man.

Glad thought our courthouse looked like it came straight out of Washington, DC, with its columns and domes. But my favorite part of the courthouse was *inside*, just behind the receptionist's desk. Here, there was a ribbon-shaped fountain, surrounded by a low brick wall, its bottom painted the aquamarine of a swimming pool. The fountain was filled with coins because *this* was the place you went when you had some serious wishing to do. Which was why I'd come here three days in a row.

Day one, I stood on the brick wall and threw a penny in the water. "I wish Bright Baby would come to life," I whispered, so the grumpy-looking woman at the receptionist's desk wouldn't hear me. But when I got home, nothing had changed. The wish had not been granted.

So day two, I threw a nickel in. "I wish Bright Baby would come to life," I said out loud, and then did a handstand on the wall when the grumpy woman wasn't looking. Still nothing. No granting.

So now, day three, I'd brought a dime. This was the plan: I'd yell, *I wish Bright Baby would come to life!* and then, before the grumpy woman could spin around in her chair, I'd hop along the fountain on one foot as fast as I could, then run out the courthouse doors.

The only problem was: I forgot the dime.

I went back outside, where the cats waited on the steps.

"Change of plans," I told them. "Right now we're going to focus on finger number two."

We headed back to the square.

Most of the shop owners knew me, since Glad's beauty parlor had been in operation for forty-eight years. Samantha had a bakery, Panis-Panis, and gave me free croissants. Nancy, the insurance agent, owned Safe and Secure, and let me help myself to her candy dish. Felix Farmer ran the antiques shop All That Is Amazing and always had anything I needed. So today, I was visiting Felix.

I'd known Felix since I was born. He and Glad had been on the Downtown Business Council together. He'd shoveled the sidewalk for her when it snowed and cranked down the beauty parlor's awning during tornado warnings. The best thing about Felix, though, was he was a cat person. When I went to All That Is Amazing, the boys didn't have to wait on the sidewalk. Felix let them come inside.

I held his shop door open, and the seven brothers paraded through, tails in the air, while Neptune and I brought up the rear.

Felix stood behind the counter, sorting through a box of salt and pepper shakers. The cats jumped up on the countertop and began to meow. They were suckers for attention.

Felix laughed. "Well, if it isn't Mercury, Venus, Earth, Mars, Jupiter, Saturn, Uranus, and Beatrice." He looked at the black kitten in my arms. "And let me guess—Neptune."

"Very good." I set Neptune on the counter.

Felix picked him up and held him to the light to examine him.

I took the opportunity to examine Felix. He was tall, with a big nose, and bald on top with a ring of short, sandy hair. He wore silver hoops in his ears. He was the same age as my mom, whom he was in love with. Before Glad died, Felix and my mom used to go bowling together, just the two of them. They were in a couples' league, and even won a giant pin-shaped trophy. Now Felix came and got his hair cut every three weeks and left a hundred-dollar tip—even though my mom cut his sideburns crooked and nicked his ears. And even though she was too *overwhelmed* to go bowling anymore.

"I would rate this kitten as being in excellent condition," Felix said. "Should I put a price tag on his collar and set him on the shelf?"

"His brothers will bite you if you do any such thing. Give him back."

Felix handed Neptune to me with a smile. Then he dug through his salt and pepper shakers and asked, "And how is your mother?" He always asked about her, since he was in love.

"Overwhelmed," I said, and walked away from the counter.

It was easy to forget your troubles inside Felix's shop, if that's what you'd come for. There were so many beautiful things to look at: china plates, marble figures, wooden statues with secret compartments. Every single item was for sale—except one: a glass bluebird hanging from a strand of fishing line in the window. In the bird's beak was a glittering piece of straw, and in its breast, a tiny ruby heart. Customers always asked about it.

"How much for the bird?" they'd say.

But Felix wouldn't sell it, not for anything. It had belonged to his mother.

I looked at the bluebird for a while, and I imagined telling Bright Baby all about it once she'd come to life. (*Glassblowing* was one of the entries in the encyclopedia.) I pictured how excited she'd be in my arms, bouncing up and down, pointing with a chubby finger at the bird. The weight of her was so real that I stumbled backward and bumped into a table. And that's when I remembered: I hadn't come to All That Is Amazing to *forget* my troubles. I'd come to *solve* them. I had to talk to Felix about my second finger.

So I went back to the counter, where Felix had lined up the salt and pepper shakers. The cats were up there, too, and Felix was stroking Saturn's and Mars's heads.

"I need a postcard."

Felix paused his stroking. "A postcard?"

"Exactly."

It had taken a lot of thought, but I'd finally come up with a way to make my second wish come true. Since I couldn't kidnap Dianne of the Flame-Red Hair, or travel back in time and stop her from moving,

I would send her a message so intriguing that she'd leave Florida and never return. In the past, I'd written letters but never received a reply. Now I'd try something shorter, something more urgent, something impossible to ignore. That's why I needed a postcard.

"I think I've got one somewhere around here." Felix disappeared behind the counter and rummaged through the shelves. When he appeared again, he had a postcard in hand. "How about this?"

Ohio: The Heart of It All! the postcard said, above a picture of a carnation, a buckeye, and a steely-eyed cardinal. "I'm not fond of the heart reference," I said, "but it will work. Do you have a pen?"

Felix handed me one from beside the cash register, then I handed him Neptune, and he and the cats watched as I wrote:

Dear D.,

I found a fossil in your old creek bed. It's absolutely SPECTACULAR, if you get my drift. If you want it, come back to Ohio FAST!

Love,

B.

"Who are you sending that to?" Felix asked.

"My best friend." I reread the postcard; it was pretty good: to the point, exciting. The only problem was, Dianne, in addition to having flame-red hair and being a genius, was also kind of stubborn. Once, I'd bet her that she couldn't stack twelve mini marshmallows on the end of her nose, and then she spent the next four hours with her eyes crossed until she'd done it. "Actually, can I have another one, in case this one doesn't do the trick?"

"The trick?" Felix asked, but he bent behind the counter, then handed me a second postcard.

It was exactly the same as the first, only on this one, the steely-eyed cardinal looked kind of doubtful. "Actually, can I have a whole bunch of postcards, like a hundred?" The more I thought about it, the more I realized Dianne was *really* stubborn. One time, in art class, our teacher said it would be impossible to re-create the *Mona Lisa* out of Froot Loops, so Dianne spent the entire year doing just that. Which meant I might have to send her a postcard every single day, to convince her to come back.

Felix laughed. "I don't have a hundred, Beatrice, but I'll give you all I have." He handed me a big stack.

"Thank you." I paused because I'd thought of something else. "Do you have any stamps?"

Felix looked at me. Sometimes, when I really missed my dad, I imagined what if *Felix* was my dad, and what if, whenever I was lonely, I just walked down to All That Is Amazing and helped him sort the salt and pepper shakers?

Sometimes I imagined that.

"Here, Beatrice. These are all the stamps currently in my possession." He handed me a whole sheet of them.

"Thank you, Mr. Farmer," I said, just for fun, since that's what Glad always called him.

Felix smiled. "It has been my absolute pleasure, Miss Corwell."

I gathered my cats. Postcard written, now I needed to find that dime. "Come on, boys," I yelled, and down the sidewalk we ran, faster than fast.

Chapter 4

I **got back to GLAD'S just before closing time. In**
the old days, I used to come in after school and
watch Glad finish up. Maybe she'd be rinsing out
a color or perming a head of hair. I liked the way she
could work without effort, chatting while she clipped,
curled, or sprayed, like doing hair was the same as
breathing. Now, though, there was never anything to
watch but my mom, customer-less, staring at the door.

The shop was empty—as usual—when the cats
and I filed in. I took a seat in one of the styling chairs.
Everywhere was purple. That was Glad's favorite
color. The sinks, the chairs, the countertops—all of
it purple. Glad said it was a soothing color and also a
rich one. When ladies saw purple, it made them want
to do expensive things to their hair.

I looked at my mom in her gold headband and purple T-shirt that was printed with the phrase *We're GLAD You're Here*. A pair of scissors was in her hand, the blades of which, you could tell, hadn't cut a single strand of hair all day. And I thought, even though I didn't want to, that Raejean-Is-Mean was right: GLAD'S was going to go out of business. The only people who stopped in were pity cuts. Like Felix, or Nancy, the insurance agent, who, after letting my mom cut her hair, walked around with a scarf on her head for a week. Occasionally, a random person would walk in off the street, but once they saw what my mom did to them, they never came back.

I kissed the top of Neptune's head. Thinking about GLAD'S closing was the most horrible of pastimes. I'd already lost Glad. There was no way I could lose her beauty parlor, too. If I had a sister, I could tell her that. Or I could tell Dianne of the Flame-Red Hair, if she were here. Dianne could sing the alphabet backward. She could paint her toenails with her eyes closed. She could divide the last doughnut in the box perfectly in half, so that both you and she got the exact same share. What I'm trying to say is: Dianne would know what to do. About GLAD'S, about Bright Baby, about everything.

"I've made some New Year's resolutions," I said.

"Resolutions are good," said my mom, though she didn't really sound like she believed it.

I decided to tell her about the message I'd found in Bright Baby's pocket. "Glad's communicating with me."

My mom looked at me from behind her glasses. "Oh, Beatrice." She started doing the breathing thing she did when she became *overwhelmed*. Deep breath in—her shoulders went up. Deep breath out—her shoulders went down.

"I don't know what she's saying yet," I continued, "because she's telling me one word at a time. I think it's because of the resolutions; that's why she's communicating. It's a reward for taking initiative. Glad was a very proactive woman."

"Beatrice, you're making me worried," my mom said in between deep breaths.

"Worried? Why would you be worried? Glad's leaving me notes again! She's going to tell me something important. Want to know what the first word is?"

"No, sweetie. Not really."

"No?" I said, shocked. "Why not?"

"I know you've been through a lot. I know how much Glad meant to you, but what you're doing isn't healthy—okay?"

"Of course it's healthy! Glad would never tell me to do something unwholesome."

"That's not what I mean," my mom said.

I shrugged. "*DO*. That's the first word."

My mom just stared.

"As in, *DO you miss me?* Not like *DEW* on the grass. Or, my library book is *DUE*. Or, I have a crooked *HAIRDO*. There are lot of *do*s, Mom. Did you know that?"

My mom closed her eyes and inhaled. "I'm familiar with the English language, sweetie, yes."

"Do you want to try to guess the next word?"

"No, Beatrice. I don't want to encourage this fantasy."

"It's not a fantasy. It's real. That's the truth and a point-blank fact. I've got the note in my dresser. Plus, the cats were there. They can back me up."

My mom sighed, and the edges of her mouth turned down. "Your cats, I'm afraid, are part of the fantasy."

My mouth fell open. "You don't think my cats are real?"

She sighed again. "Of course they're real—but not in the way you pretend."

"What's that supposed to mean?" I asked suspiciously.

"You act like they have human brains."

I laughed out loud. I knew my cats didn't have human brains. A human brain wouldn't even fit inside a cat's skull.

"Plus, there are too many of them," my mom added.

I didn't laugh that time. Now she was trying to pick a fight. Well, I didn't feel like fighting, not in front of Neptune, who was young and impressionable. (I'd read about *psychological development* in the encyclopedia.) So I bit my tongue and stared at the big photo of my face hanging on the wall.

I was five in the picture, and Glad had curled my hair. My eyes sparkled. I had a lopsided grin. The five-year-old me looked so happy, with a big bow on top of her head, that the ten-year-old me became kind of angry, angry that she got to live in a time when Glad was alive. Angry that she'd never had to think about being made of tin.

"Who does she think she is?" I didn't mean to say it out loud.

"Who does *who* think she is?" my mom asked.

"Oh, I was just talking to myself," I said, not realizing till the words came out how funny that was because I really was *talking to myself.*

"Beatrice," my mom said.

The bell above the door rang just then.

We both turned. My mom stood up, her scissors

snipping the air. We had a customer! An actual customer. I was so excited that I forgot to pull a bead.

And then I saw who it was.

"Oh, good grief," I mumbled.

Neptune let out a disappointed squeak.

There, in the doorway, stood Caleb Chernavachin.

"Where's Glad?" he said loudly. "I need a haircut."

"Glad is deceased, so I'll be cutting your hair today," my mom said. "My name's Marta. Please, have a seat." She gestured toward a purple styling chair.

Caleb stayed where he was. He had on the too-small coat and a pair of jeans with a ripped knee. "Looks like you got the cat out," he said to me.

"That's correct." I snuggled Neptune closer to my chest.

"I guess I'll get my haircut here," Caleb said to my mom, "but you should know my dad's a famous wrestler, so I have high standards."

"I'll do my best." My mom fastened a purple cape around his neck once he'd climbed into the chair. "What can I do for you today?"

"Just kinda trim it up," Caleb said.

I stared at his reflection: the round face, the freckles, the porcupine quills. His hair was already so ridiculous that my mom couldn't make it any worse.

"I'm rich," Caleb told her.

"That must be nice." My mom took her scissors to the side of his head.

"If I ask for a quarter, my mom gives me a hundred-dollar bill."

"Yeah, right," I said, without planning to.

My mom gave me a disappointed look in the mirror, like I'd just told her best customer he smelled like a moldy shoe.

"She don't believe me!" Caleb said, pointing a finger at my reflection.

"Beatrice has always been a bit of a skeptic," my mom said. Then she raised an eyebrow and added, "About some things."

"What's that supposed to mean?" I asked.

"Nothing," my mom said, snip-snipping Caleb's hair.

I made my face as mean as I could and scowled at the back of my mom's head.

Caleb saw me. "Someone's been drinkin' grump juice."

"Looks like someone's been drinking *a lot* of grump juice," my mom added.

Oh, how they laughed then, like a couple of hyenas. But I didn't soften my gaze even a smidge because I don't give in to peer pressure.

"There," my mom said. "All done." She whipped

the cape off Caleb like a magician revealing a lady he'd sawed in half. "What do you think?"

Caleb leaned forward in the chair and studied his reflection. "It's different, but I like it."

"Ridiculous," I whispered into the top of Neptune's head. Caleb's hair looked the same. Maybe a millimeter shorter, but that was it.

My mom went over to the cash register. "That'll be ten dollars."

Caleb stood in the middle of the beauty parlor, a big toe poking out of the hole in his sneaker. He pulled a freckled earlobe. "I don't have any money."

GLAD'S was very quiet then. I could hear the padding of the cats' feet on the linoleum. I looked down at Neptune's sweet little face. He blinked, and I think I heard that, too.

"What about the hundred-dollar bill from your mom?" I finally asked.

Caleb pulled his other earlobe. "I forgot it."

"How about you just pay me next time?" my mom said.

"Are you kidding me?" I asked. "You cut his hair. He's got to pay you. If he doesn't, he's a thief."

"I'm no thief," Caleb shouted, "you crooked-haired cat-girl!"

"You want to see a cat-girl? I'll show you a cat-girl," I said—and then I called them. *"Here, kitty-kitty-kitty."*

I said it super high and super fast. No cat could resist that call. And here my boys came, leaping from their hiding spots. They lined up, three on my right, three on my left, with Mercury right in front of me. Being the oldest, he was sort of the leader. (I'd read about *alpha animals* in the encyclopedia.)

"That's a lot of cats," Caleb said.

I could tell he was nervous.

But then my mom said, "I think things have gotten off on the wrong foot. I'd like to fix that. Join us for dinner—okay?"

The cats and I gasped.

Caleb smiled. "I'm hungry as a hippopotamus!"

So that's how I was forced to eat pork chops and French fries with the most ridiculous boy in the universe.

Chapter 5

"Beatrice, you can show our guest around while I make dinner—okay?" my mom said as we climbed the stairs to our apartment.

It was dark out—the sun set at five o'clock now—and the Christmas tree in the traffic circle glowed. Seeing it made me think of things I didn't want to think of.

"He's not a guest. He's Caleb Chernavachin."

"Then show Caleb Chernavachin around."

"That will take five seconds."

"Make it take longer." She unlocked the door. The cats raced ahead of us, which was bad manners, but it's hard to teach cats to wait in line. *No buts, no cuts, no coconuts* just doesn't have any meaning for them.

"My house is *way* bigger than this," Caleb said. "I live in a mansion."

I rolled my eyes. "You already told me that."

"No, I didn't."

I couldn't remember if he'd actually said the mansion part, but it *seemed* like something he'd say.

"Why don't you show Caleb your room?" my mom said on her way to the kitchen.

The cats ran ahead again. They loved having visitors, even if the visitors in question were porcupine-headed thieves.

I took Caleb to my room. He saw my solar system bedspread, and poster of the constellations, and hanging mobile of the moon.

"I bet you wanna be an astronaut."

"I personally have no interest in space, but my cats do."

He looked at me and squinted, like he was trying to read some writing that was very, very small. Then he said, "Beatrice, you are a mystery."

I smiled because I liked that. I'd rather be a mystery than an astronaut.

"Just you and your mom live here?" he asked.

I nodded.

"Where's your dad?"

I brought Neptune up to my face and kissed his

kitten mouth. "Antarctica." Since I hadn't seen my dad since I was eight, there was a possibility this was true.

Caleb's eyes got big. "What's he doing *there*?"

"Catching penguins." This also might be true. If my dad was in Antarctica, there wouldn't be much else for him to do. Trust me—I'd read all about *Antarctica* in the encyclopedia.

"What for?"

"Meat," I said.

Caleb stared at me. Then he said, "Aw, you're lyin'." But I could tell he wasn't sure if I was.

"You know a lot about lying, huh? Mr. Hundred-Dollar Bill."

Caleb shrugged in his too-small coat. "You're just jealous," he said—which was exactly what Raejean-Is-Mean had said earlier.

I eyed him suspiciously. "Do you know Raejean?"

"I only know famous people. Is she famous?" Instead of waiting for an answer, he began to look around my room. He went over to the bookshelf, opened the dresser drawers, stuck his head in the closet.

The cats were all on my bed, and they gave me a look that meant, *Do you want us to stop him?* I motioned for them to remain where they were. I was in the process of training them to attack, like dogs, but

I hadn't had a chance to test them yet. And I didn't think Caleb would be the right person to start with. My mom would be furious if he came to dinner covered in scratches.

"Hey, what's this?" Caleb had discovered my jewelry box. He opened the lid. "You only got one thing!"

That was the truth and a point-blank fact. In my jewelry box was a ring. It had a gold band, and affixed to the band was a flower made of jewels: opal petals with specks of rubies and emeralds. The center was a diamond.

"Whoa. This must be worth a lot of money." Caleb held the ring up to the light.

"Maybe." It was Glad's engagement ring. My mom gave it to me after she died, which meant the ring was valuable whether it was worth any money or not.

Caleb put the ring back. "What else you got to show me?"

"I could show you Glad's room."

"I thought Glad was dead."

"She is."

"Did she die in her room?"

I nodded, remembering all the evenings I'd sat by her bedside as her soul slowly slipped far, far away. Going . . . going . . . until finally, she'd gone.

"That means it's haunted."

"Glad's not a ghost," I said.

Caleb leaned back on his heels, unconvinced. "What was she like?"

That was the worst question anybody could ask. What was Glad like? She was like the person you walked with along the river, carrying a bag of bird-seed for the geese. She was like the one who took you shopping for back-to-school shoes with a scoop of mint-chocolate-chip ice cream afterward. She was like the one who'd tuck a drawing in your lunch box of a squiggly-lined person with a speech balloon saying, *I love you!*

But now she was like nothing. She was the person a million-billion miles away whose face you couldn't see. The hate I felt for that fact made me want to burst into tears. My heart was just too stinking bumpy.

I clenched my eyes tight and pulled three beads in my pocket.

"I didn't mean to make you cry," said Caleb.

"I wasn't crying." I wiped my nose. Luckily, no tears had escaped. There was nothing worse than having an emotional breakdown in front of some ridiculous boy.

"Come on," I said, and led him to Glad's room.

I turned on the light and smiled at the sight of Bright Baby, resting on the comforter. It was impossible not to smile when I saw her because it was impossible not to imagine her come to life, kicking and cooing in the middle of the bed. And imagining her come to life made me remember: I hadn't thrown the dime in the fountain!

"Oh no," I said.

The cats looked at me, and so did Caleb.

"What's wrong?" he asked.

"I have to go somewhere." I ran down the hall, to my bedroom.

"Can I come, too?" called Caleb.

"If you hurry," I yelled back.

I set Neptune on my mattress and crawled under my bed and found a dime. Then I raced into the kitchen, where my mom was at the stove.

"Keep it warm till I get back," I said, then ran out the door. Behind me, Caleb clomped down the stairs.

"Wait for me!"

But I couldn't wait. There wasn't time. If you want to make your wishes come true, you can't slow down. You have to chase them, faster than fast.

I ran across the traffic circle with Caleb puffing behind me. I finally reached the courthouse just as the grumpy-faced woman was locking the doors.

"Building's closed," she said.

"Please," I pleaded, "can I go inside, just for a second? There's a wish I need to make. It's of utmost urgency."

"A wish?" she said, as if she'd never heard of such a thing, as if a wishing fountain weren't located just behind her desk.

"It's about my sister."

She looked at Caleb.

"That's not my sister. That's Caleb Chernavachin."

The grumpy woman sighed. "Fine. But make it quick. One wish."

"Oh, thank you!" I ran into the courthouse, with Caleb bumbling after me.

Once I got to the fountain, I climbed onto the wall and closed my eyes.

"What's your wish?" Caleb asked.

"Shh." I took a deep breath. "I wish Bright Baby would come to life!" I yelled, and reached into my pocket to retrieve the dime—but the dime wasn't there.

"Oh no."

"What's wrong?" Caleb climbed onto the wall beside me.

"I lost my dime. It must have fallen out of my pocket."

"What do you need a dime for?"

"You can't make a wish at a fountain without any money," I explained impatiently. Then I tried to think. There was no way the grumpy woman would let me go home and get another dime. Maybe if I—

"I got an idea. Get a dime out of there." Caleb pointed to the center of the fountain, where the other coins had accumulated.

"I can't use those. They've already been wished on."

"So?"

"So, you can't wish on a wished-on dime. It's been used."

Caleb shook his head. "Nah. The wishes wear off after they've floated in the water for a couple hours. Those dimes are good as new."

I stared at the coins at the bottom of the fountain. Did wishes really wear off, or was Caleb lying again? If only Dianne were here. In first grade, when Courtney Cartman handed me a golden rock and said it was worth a million dollars, Dianne's the one who told me about pyrite. And that same year, when Dori Dartlinger claimed her hair was actually a wig, Dianne taught me how to rub my scalp back and forth so my hair looked like a wig, too. Dianne was the equivalent of three encyclopedia sets. She of the Flame-Red Hair would know the truth.

"Anyway," I said to Caleb, "even if I wanted to use one, I can't reach it. I don't have extendable arms."

"You don't need extendable arms, goofball. You just gotta get in."

"It's a fountain, not a swimming pool, goofhead. I can't *get in*."

"Sure you can." And without taking off his shoes or rolling up his pants, Caleb jumped into the fountain. "See?" He sloshed through the water and picked up a handful of coins. "How many do you want?"

I was speechless.

"Here, just take them all." He dumped the coins into my hands. Then he climbed out of the fountain and returned to his spot beside me, soaking wet. "Go on," he said.

And so, since Dianne wasn't here and I didn't know what else to do, I cleared my throat and yelled: "I wish Bright Baby would come to life!" Then I threw the whole handful of coins into the water and hopped on one foot all the way around the wall, till I got back to where I started.

"Finished," I said.

And Caleb, who'd just gone swimming fully clothed in the courthouse fountain, had the audacity to say, "That, Beatrice, was the weirdest thing I ever saw."

Chapter 6

"So who's Bright Baby?" Caleb asked as we walked back to my apartment.

"Bright gravy? I love gravy. How about you?" (I'd read about *obfuscation techniques* in the encyclopedia.)

"Bright *Baby*," said Caleb, who had not been obfuscated.

I looked at him, soaking wet, with icicles forming on his pants. I didn't want to tell him about Bright Baby—I'd never told *anyone* about Bright Baby, not even Dianne of the Flame-Red Hair—but I kind of owed him, since he'd jumped into the fountain so I could make my wish.

"Can you keep a secret?"

Caleb nodded, looking more untrustworthy than ever.

I took a shaky breath. "You know the doll lying on Glad's bed?"

"The real spooky one?"

"She's not spooky!" I shoved his wet back.

Caleb scowled. "Fine. You mean the *not*-spooky one?"

"Yes." I paused, not knowing if I dared. I wished I'd brought the boys along; they were good judges of character. "Well, that's Bright Baby," I finally said. "I want her to come to life and be my baby sister."

Caleb was quiet.

"Kind of weird, huh?" I asked.

"Nah. I've wished weirder things than that." He pulled an earlobe, thinking. "So that's why you're goin' to the fountain?"

"It's my New Year's resolution. One of them."

He nodded, thinking again. Then he said, "Well, I gotta tell you somethin'."

"What?"

"If you want that doll to come to life, you're gonna need more than a fountain."

We'd come to the Christmas tree in the traffic circle and stopped beside its glowing branches.

"What do you mean?"

"What you need is *magic*."

I put my hands on my hips. "Fountains *are* magic."

"I mean, like, *strong* magic." Caleb started walking again, and I followed him. The daylight was nearly all gone now, so it was like I was chasing a shadow. "What you need is my granny."

We paused at the bottom of the staircase, just outside GLAD'S.

"How could your granny help?"

"She's a witch."

I looked at him, to see if he was teasing—but his face was solemn as a tree stump. Maybe I'd misheard. "A *what*?"

"A witch—you know."

I didn't know. Maybe when Caleb said *witch*, he really meant *firefighter* or *librarian*. "You mean with a broom and pointy hat?"

"Don't be stupid," he said.

I shoved him in the back again. *I* wasn't being stupid. *He* was the one who said his granny was a witch.

"She could cast a come-to-life spell—or somethin' like that."

"Yeah, right."

"I'm serious!"

"Well, I don't believe you."

Caleb scowled again.

And I thought of Bright Baby, resting peacefully on Glad's bed. Even if Caleb wasn't lying, there was no way I'd let his wart-nosed granny cast a spell on her. "Never," I said just as the apartment door opened above us.

"Dinner!" my mom called.

I ran up the staircase and scooped up Neptune. Then all ten of us—me, the boys, and Caleb—went to the dining room table.

Caleb sat at the head, since he was the guest. He still had on his coat, and his shirtsleeves were wet up to the elbows, but my mom didn't seem to notice. She and I sat on either side of him, and the cats filled the rest of the chairs, doubling up on some of them. I put Neptune in a salad spinner lined with a dish towel and set him in the center of the table.

There was a plate of pork chops and a bowl of French fries. Caleb helped himself without waiting to be asked, grabbing food like it was bars of gold.

"You got any ketchup?" he said as he picked up a slab of pork and tore into it like a barbarian.

The cats looked at me, horrified by the boy's lack of manners.

I shrugged, as if to say, *Our guest eats like a wild hog. What can you do?* Then I turned to Neptune, the cutest lettuce you'd ever seen, sitting there in the salad spinner. And I thought of the rule of three. Two of the three somebodies I was to meet were sitting right here at the table. But the third was still missing.

Where are you? I wondered. *I'm waiting.*

Then I froze as a shiver slid up my spine, showering goose bumps across my skin.

Far away, somewhere out in the night, rattled the cold, cruel cackle of a witch.

Chapter 7

The Christmas tree in the town square came down the next day, and I went back to school. The cats walked me to Kolbe Elementary with their bows on, tails up. All except Neptune, who was too little for the expedition, and so stayed behind with Bright Baby.

"Someone to keep you company," I told her that morning, and set him beside her on the bed. Then I slung my backpack over my shoulder and headed off to *The Place That Was and Always Would Be*. That's what I called school.

Nothing interesting ever happened there. The cats knew I'd rather be anywhere else, so they always thought up ways to get me to skip class. Especially Earth, the rebellious blue-gray domestic shorthair.

He'd climb trees and hide under cars, trying to get me to spend the whole morning searching for him. Sometimes he succeeded, and then my mom would be so mad when the principal called that she'd threaten to take Earth to the pound. She never did, which I'm happy about—but it's also why he hadn't learned his lesson.

Today, though, I made it to *The Place That Was and Always Would Be* with only a handful of distractions. First Earth jumped into the back of an open mail truck, and I had to pull him out by his hind legs. Then Mars got his head stuck inside an empty ravioli can, and I had to use my lip balm to grease his neck in order to pull the can off. But other than that, the walk was uneventful. When we reached the building, I told the cats to wait for me in the grass, along the bank of homeroom windows. Then I squared my shoulders and went inside.

Raejean stood by the lockers. She made a face with her teeth sticking out, like a beaver, so I made a face like a wolf. At least, I hoped it was a wolf face. Animal impressions are hard to do without a mirror. Caleb sat in a desk in the front row. He was so absorbed in pulling dried glue from his palm that he didn't notice me. I took a seat at my desk in the back. The bell rang, then the boringness began.

Reading, writing, spelling. You turned in a math quiz and got an A. You wrote a poem and the teacher thought it was so good she made you recite it for the class. On your lunch tray appeared a scoopful of peas, every single one of them dented. The odds of this naturally occurring were zero—I'd read about *probabilities* in the encyclopedia—which meant the cooks had purposefully dropped the cans.

School was the same thing over and over again. That's the truth and a point-blank fact. At least now I had something to help me pass the time.

I slipped an *Ohio: The Heart of It All!* postcard from my desk and studied the steely-eyed cardinal, whose beak looked especially pointy today. Then I turned the postcard over and wrote:

Dear D.,
Just to be clear: the fossil is PRISTINE.
Also, it's from the Cambrian period. Hint, hint!
But that's all I'm going to say. If you want
to find out more, COME TO OHIO AT ONCE!
Love,
B.

I reread the postcard, reveling in its perfection, then slipped it back into my desk before Mrs. Hartley could see it. One wish taken care of for the day, one more to go.

I stared at Caleb Chernavachin's porcupine head, which was big and round, two facts you couldn't help noticing when you sat in the back row. The question was, *Is Caleb's fat, round porcupine head full of anything besides lies?* What I wondered, as Mrs. Hartley wrote *predicate adjective* on the board, was, *Is it possible that a big lying liar might know something about magic? For example, are fountains really too weak to grant wishes?* There was no way Caleb's granny was an actual witch—that was a lie, one hundred percent—but maybe that ridiculous boy was right about needing something more than a fountain to make Bright Baby come to life. I opened my notebook and wrote *Things to Wish On* at the top. I thought for a moment, then scribbled:

Fountains
First stars
Birthday candles

I kept thinking until, finally, the bell rang, at which point I raced out of the building faster than fast.

The cats were happy to see me, rubbing against

my legs and meowing. After nearly three weeks of vacation, they weren't used to my being gone all day. "I missed you, too," I said. "Let's get out of here."

They lined up, and away we marched.

I peeked in the GLAD'S shop window when we reached the building. Nancy, the insurance agent, was in a styling chair, getting her monthly pity cut. She looked worried as my mom applied something frothy to her hair. She'd brought along her poodle, Sprinkles, for a bath because she said no one could make that stinky dog smell as good as my mom could.

After we waved to Sprinkles, the cats and I raced upstairs. We paused to look at the pile of mail on the kitchen table, but there was nothing from a girl with flame-red hair. So we ran through the apartment, all thirty of our feet pounding the floor.

"Bright Baby! Neptune! We're here!"

When I saw them in the bedroom, sleeping in a beam of sunlight, my heart swelled like a balloon. For a moment, I forgot all about the Tin Man Project and just let myself feel the goodness of the two of them. Then I scooped up Neptune and pulled the chair over to the bed.

"The first day back is always the hardest," I told Bright Baby. I pressed Neptune's fat little belly against my mouth, breathing in his sweet kitten smell. "But we'll get into the swing of things. It'll get easier. Don't worry."

I set Neptune on the floor, then looked toward the window, where light poured in, in a golden mist. I imagined Glad floating in a pool of shimmering water, which is how I pictured heaven. And then I decided to speak to her, in my mind, because that was the only way she'd be able to hear me. Voices can't travel to a place a million-billion miles away, but thoughts—they're different. Thoughts float and linger. They sweep through the air, in gusty swirls.

I'm ready when you are, I said, trying to push the words in my mind out the window and through the golden mist. I stole a peek at Bright Baby's pocket.

It was flat, which meant empty.

So I added, *For your next word*, in case Glad didn't know what I'd meant.

Another peek: the pocket was flat as ever.

I can tell you the first word, in case you forgot.

On Earth, Glad's memory had been in tip-top shape, but who knew what condition it was in now.

DO, I reminded her. *Not DEW. Or DUE. But DO.*

I closed my eyes and counted to ten because sometimes that makes things happen. When I opened them again, Bright Baby's eyes were open, too. I jumped from my chair and slipped two fingers into her lace pocket.

NOT was what was written on the slip of paper.

I looked at Bright Baby, who had reclosed her eyes. "DO NOT—" I said out loud. "DO NOT—DO NOT *what*?"

DO NOT believe in Granny Witch?

"Don't worry, Glad," I whispered. "Not a chance."

The Place That Was and Always Would Be ate up my time slowly. *Crunch, crunch, crunch* went the days, then *chew, chew, chew.* I was lonely at school. I didn't have any friends. Which was why it was so inconsiderate of Dianne of the Flame-Red Hair to move to Florida. I told her that, too, on the day we said goodbye, standing in her gravel driveway beside the moving truck.

"Best friends don't move a thousand miles away," I said.

Dianne sighed and re-ponytailed her hair. She had on palm tree sunglasses and an *I Love Florida* T-shirt. "I keep telling you, Beatrice, I don't have a choice. My dad got a new job. I *have* to move."

"We'll never see each other again."

"I'll write you," she said, as if getting a letter from somebody was the same as catching crawdads with them in a creek.

"I don't want your letters," I said. "I want *you*."

"Well, I'm sorry, Beatrice, but you can't have me." Her voice sounded sad.

So I grabbed her by the arms and pulled her to me, hugging her tighter than tight. I hugged her like, if I pressed hard enough, I could absorb her into my body and carry her around forever.

Then I watched the moving truck drive away and instantly regretted what I'd said about the letters. I *did* want her letters; I wanted every single one of them. Even the ones that just said, *Hi, B. Love, D.*

So that's one more way you can miss somebody. You can miss the crisp white envelope you might have held in your hand.

The Place That Was and Always Would Be was mind-numbingly dull without Dianne. But I tried to make the best of it. I worked on my resolutions; I took action; I kept my initiative.

Dear D.,

Knowing you, you're probably thinking: "I don't need Beatrice's fossil. I'll dig up a fossil of my own." Let me be blunt: fat chance. This

particular fossil is very rare. You'd have
better luck sailing down the river on a tube
of toothpaste than you would finding another
fossil like this one. So come and get it while
the getting's good. (And the getting, don't
forget, is in OHIO.)

Love,
B.

I didn't abandon the fountain. Every day, after
checking the mail, I went there, threw in my coin,
then performed a physical feat—a crab walk, a snake
crawl, a rooster strut. But every day, when I got home,
still no sister. The grumpy-faced woman was sick of
seeing me, and I was sick of seeing her.

So I decided to try something else from the list. I
sat by my window, waiting for the first star to appear.
But since I lived downtown, with lots of streetlamps,
I didn't see any stars, just airplanes and UFOs. Still,
I said the poem, right when the first star *would have*
appeared, had I been able to see it:

"Star light, star bright,
First star I see tonight,
I wish I may, I wish I might,
Let Bright Baby come to life!"

Nothing happened. I was in what Glad would call a *rut*.

So one day, at *The Place That Was and Always Would Be*, instead of racing outside faster than fast when the bell rang, I stood up and moved slower than slow. That's how I ended up in the hallway with Caleb. I still hadn't decided how much he knew about magic, but what I was doing wasn't working, which meant it was time for a change of plans.

"What about a birthday cake?" I asked.

He stared at me in his too-small coat. "What about it?"

"That's got magic, right, when you blow out the candles?"

He pulled his earlobe. "Not as much as a witch."

"I know it's not as much as a witch—duh!" I said. "But is it *enough*?"

Caleb lifted his chin and pressed his lips together, as if to really think about it. "I doubt it," he finally said. "But you could try."

"Good. I will."

"Is today your birthday?"

"No."

"Then how are you gonna get a cake?"

That, unfortunately, was a good question. "I'm not sure."

"Hold on. I got somethin'." Caleb took off his backpack and set it on the ground. "It's gotta be in here somewhere," he said, digging around. "Here!" He handed me a half-eaten muffin in a dirty wrapper.

I recoiled both on the inside and the out. *"What is that?"*

"A birthday cake."

"That's not a cake. That's a half-eaten muffin!"

"It's all I got!" Caleb yelled.

Regrettably, it was all I had, too. "Fine. Do you have a candle?"

He dug around some more in his backpack. "Nope."

That was the answer I'd expected because there's only so much you can hope for from a ridiculous boy. Luckily, I knew someone who always had what you needed, inside the most amazing store.

It was time to see the Farmer known as Felix.

Chapter 8

When Caleb and I stepped outside, the cats were in a tizzy. Maybe they were excited to see the ridiculous boy again. Maybe they were looking forward to the weekend. Whatever the reason, they were determined to lead *me* home, instead of my leading them. And I let them, so they could practice their independence. The nine of us walked down the sidewalk, with Caleb and me at the rear.

When we came to All That Is Amazing, I told the cats to stop.

"This is where the candles are," I told Caleb, then opened the door.

"Mercury, Venus, Earth, Mars, Jupiter, Saturn, Uranus, and Beatrice—so good to see you," Felix said from behind the counter. He was sorting through a box of toothpick holders. My boys jumped up to help him. "Where's Neptune?"

"At home," I said.

Felix turned to Caleb. "I don't believe we've had the pleasure of meeting."

"This is Caleb Chernavachin," I said.

"Nice to meet you, Caleb Chernavachin. I'm Felix Farmer." He stuck out his hand.

Caleb shook it. "I'm real rich." He looked around at the shelves. "You sure got a lot of junk in here."

I elbowed his puffy-coated ribs. "Don't call it *junk*."

Felix laughed. "He can call it whatever he wants. Now, how can I help you two today?"

"I need a candle," I said, holding up the half-eaten muffin, "for my birthday cake."

Felix looked at me, and I looked at him. He was the kind of person who, when you called something what it obviously wasn't, didn't laugh in your face. I was happy about that.

"I must have a candle around here somewhere." He bent down behind the counter. "Voilà!" he announced a few seconds later. Then he bowed and held it out for me to take from his hand.

I did and poked it into the muffin. "How about a match?"

"One moment." He disappeared again and, a moment later, had a book of matches. "Shall I light it?"

"Please do."

Felix did. "So whom are we singing to?"

"Her." Caleb pointed in my direction.

Felix raised his eyebrows. "It's *your* birthday, Beatrice?"

"Sort of. Not really."

"Strange answer, but . . ." Felix took a deep breath before belting out: *"Happy birthday to you . . ."*

Caleb joined in, and I closed my eyes, preparing for the moment when the singing stopped.

When it did, I cried out silently, *I wish Bright Baby would come to life!* Then I blew the candle on that half-eaten muffin with as much energy as I could muster.

"Bravo!" Felix cried. "Who wants the first slice?"

"Not me," Caleb said. "You can have the whole thing, Beatrice."

"Thanks, I guess." I set the muffin on the counter, where the cats took turns sniffing it.

Caleb leaned in close. "If this don't work, and you change your mind about my granny helpin' you, let me know." Then he turned and left.

"Mr. Farmer," I asked when we were alone, "if a person told you his grandma was a witch, would you believe him?"

Felix scratched Uranus's chin. "I suppose if he offered some sort of proof, Miss Corwell, I might."

I thought about that for a minute. "Say he did prove it. Would you ask the witch for help?"

Felix stopped scratching. "I would only seek a witch's assistance in the most desperate of circumstances."

I nodded.

"Is there something bothering you, Beatrice?"

Not a care in the world is what I planned to tell him, in a most Tin Man–like fashion, but when I opened my mouth, what came out was, "My dad always comes to visit in the even years, but I've been ten since April, and now it's the end of January, which means he's running out of time."

Felix looked at me, and I looked at him. He seemed as shocked by my words as I was. I'd been so focused on two of my wishes that I thought I'd forgotten about the other three. But obviously, I hadn't. Those other wishes were still there, lurking beneath the surface, just waiting for a chance to pop out when I was least expecting it.

"I'm sorry to hear that," Felix finally said, as if I'd just told him my dad had died.

And maybe he *had* died. Maybe that's why he hadn't come to visit. Maybe he was in Antarctica, frozen in a block of ice, with a waddle of penguins huddled on top of his carcass. (I'd read about *hypothermia* in the encyclopedia.)

"I think I could use a haircut," Felix said, out of the blue.

I looked at him. His hair didn't need trimming. That's the truth and a point-blank fact. But when you're in love with a woman who works in a beauty parlor, you'll pay for unnecessary services.

"Mind if I walk with you to GLAD'S?"

"Sure. But just so you know, the cats are leading today."

"Got it." He locked the shop door.

We walked down the street. At the corner, we turned by the traffic circle. And then we stopped.

Sprawled on the sidewalk in front of GLAD'S was a person wearing a purple *We're GLAD You're Here* T-shirt.

Chapter 9

I screamed, I think. I know I ran. And then I was crouched on the sidewalk beside my mom, her hand grabbing my wrist so tightly I thought she'd break my bones.

"Marta, what happened?" Felix asked.

My mom did her breathing thing. Deep breath in . . . deep breath out . . . *"Overwhelmed,"* she whispered.

"Oh, Mom!" I wailed, even though Tin Men don't wail. They moan when their joints get stiff from a lack of oil, but that's it.

My mom closed her eyes and released a long, ragged breath.

A car stopped on the street. "You need some help?" the driver yelled.

"We're okay," Felix called. Then he said, "Let's get you inside, Marta," and pulled my mom up with both hands and guided her toward the stairs.

"Come on, boys," I said, and we trooped after them.

Inside the apartment, Felix helped my mom get settled on the futon. He wrapped a blanket around her shoulders, boiled water for tea, then ordered a pizza.

"Thank you," she said, holding the mug between her hands. "You're a good friend."

Felix smiled. "Whatever you need, Marta. I'm always just around the corner."

My mom had fallen asleep under her blanket when the pizza arrived, so Felix and I ate it with the cats at the table. We gave them each a slice of pepperoni, which, for felines, is the equivalent of a banana split.

"Now what?" Felix asked after we'd cleared the table.

"Want to make something?"

"As long as it's spectacular."

I got out a pad of construction paper, and we made paper crowns. Then we lined up the cats.

"Beautiful!" Felix said after we attached a crown to each cat's head. "Too bad they can't do anything."

I felt offended. "They can do all sorts of things."

"Like what?"

"Walk in a straight line and come when called."

"That's nothing," Felix scoffed. "Dogs can do that."

"I'm teaching them to attack, like dogs."

"No." Felix shook his bald head. "They should do something inherent to their feline nature."

I had no idea what he meant.

"Hmm." He studied each cat, eyes squinted, appraising. Then he said, "I know! Dancing."

"*Dancing?* Are you serious?"

"Very."

I looked at the cats. "Do you want Felix to teach you how to dance?"

Their eyes shone with excitement. Each one nodded yes. Even Neptune, who I don't think knew what *dance* meant.

Felix grinned. "Then let's get started."

We spent the rest of the night teaching the cats to dance. Felix had a thing he did with his hand, where he wiggled it like a fish. He lined the cats up in two rows, then said, "The fish swims this way."

The cats stepped to the right.

"The fish swims that way."

The cats stepped to the left.

"The fish swims far."

They stepped backward.

"The fish swims near."

They stepped forward.

Then Felix said, "A worm is on the hook."

They swished their tails and meowed.

It was exhausting, trying to keep them in formation, luring them back with bits of canned tuna when they became discouraged and left. Finally, after many hours, the dance was perfected. Felix and I collapsed at the table.

"Now what?" he asked.

I glanced at my mom, who was still asleep and breathing normally, on the couch.

"Have you ever seen that show? The one where people find stuff in their attics, then ask a person to tell them how much it's worth?"

Felix smiled. "It's my favorite."

"Do you want to play it?"

"You mean—you bring me something, and I appraise it?"

"Exactly." I ran to my room to get the one valuable thing I owned. Ever since Caleb had asked, I'd been curious. How much was the flower ring worth?

I handed it to Felix. He looked at it carefully, turning it over in his palm. "Five thousand dollars." He handed it back to me. "Don't wear it to school."

"I won't." I slipped it on my finger. "I only wear it

at home. If something were to happen to it, it'd be more than I could bear."

Felix nodded. "That's exactly how I feel about my bluebird. Who gave you the ring?"

"Glad."

"I bet you miss her."

I nodded. I missed Glad so much that sometimes it felt like there was nothing left of me *but* the missing. It was the same with Dianne of the Flame-Red Hair. I just missed and missed and kept on missing her. Missing is not a thing you can ever run out of. That's the truth and a point-blank fact. Glad was a million-billion miles away, and I'd never see her earthly form again. Dianne was only a thousand miles from me, but unless I could write a postcard most persuasive, I'd never see her again, either.

"You want to know who else I miss?" I asked. "My dad."

I don't know why I told him that. I don't know why I started thinking about dads every time I was with Felix.

"The way I miss him is different from the way I miss Glad, though. I've only seen him four times, so there's not a lot to miss. But what I *do* miss are the things we would've done together—if my dad was here. He's running out of time," I added, "if he wants to see me on an even birth year."

"I know, Beatrice," Felix said quietly. "You told me."

"Oh, Felix," I blurted out, "sometimes I wish *you* were my dad."

I shouldn't have. Some wishes aren't meant to be spoken or counted on your fingers. Some wishes are too fragile to exist anywhere except inside your head.

Felix's face turned red. "Well . . . if your mom . . . I mean, I'd like to, but . . . um . . ."

Everything was awkward then. "I have to go to the bathroom," I announced, even though I didn't. I left Felix at the table, stroking Mercury's tail.

In Glad's room, the curtains were drawn, so the light was dim, but I could make out Bright Baby, who was ghostly gray in the shadows. If she were my sister, the embarrassing thing I told Felix wouldn't matter. None of it would matter. I'd be too busy changing diapers and filling bottles to care. There'd be warm baths to draw and jars of food to rinse and the tiniest teeth to brush. What I'm trying to say is, if Bright Baby came to life, everything broken would be fixed.

But she hadn't come to life.

Caleb was right: birthday-wish magic wasn't strong enough.

I touched Bright Baby's pocket, which was empty.

Not today, huh, Glad? Then I stood at the dresser and thought. Caleb was a liar, but just because someone tells lies doesn't mean they *never* tell the truth. Maybe his granny *was* a witch. Maybe, if I asked, he could prove it.

But, on the other hand, Bright Baby was so innocent. Even if Caleb did prove it was true, a part of me didn't want his wart-nosed granny to come near her. Besides, Felix said you should only contact a witch if your circumstances were desperate.

Here was the thing, though: I *was* desperate. Everyone had left: Glad, Dianne, my dad. The apartment was you're-all-alone-in-the-world empty. But if Bright Baby were alive, she'd fill some of that emptiness. She'd crawl in the hallway and splash in the tub and pull my hair. Bright Baby would be a *fullness*, like a whole *circle* of moon, instead of just a sliver.

I had to make her come to life. I just *had to*. The problem was: I couldn't find a magic strong enough.

But *somebody* could.

I shivered at the thought of that somebody, who maybe, right now, was watching me in her crystal ball.

Then I went back to the living room, where Felix still sat at the table. His face was no longer red. The cats had surrounded him, and he was trying to pet them all at once.

"I'm going to get some fresh air," I said.

"Outside? It's dark."

"I won't go far." I grabbed my coat and ran down the stairs, faster than fast.

I stood on the street corner and stared at the empty spot where the Christmas tree had been. Cars drove by, their headlights shining in the night. I wondered if Granny Witch's crystal ball could see me in all this blackness.

"Hey," a voice said from behind. "Whatcha lookin' at?"

It was Caleb. I could just make out his figure in that too-small coat.

"Bright Baby didn't come to life," I said.

"*Now* do you want me to ask my granny to help you?"

I stared at the empty traffic circle. The Christmas tree was another thing that had left, and that leaving made the world feel emptier than ever. I pulled a bead in my pocket.

"Is she *really* a witch?"

"Yep."

"Can you *prove* it?"

"Uh-huh."

"How?"

"Soon as you see her, you'll know it's true."

I imagined Granny Witch in a long black dress, stirring a cauldron with one hand while a crooked finger on the other beckoned me to come near. I pictured a tall, peak-roofed house whose porch was lined with gargoyles and sleeping bats. "Is your granny a good witch or a bad witch?"

Caleb spit on the sidewalk. "There's only one kind of witch, Beatrice."

My heart fluttered. How I hated that it was muscle instead of tin.

"You want me to ask her?" he repeated.

I closed my eyes. I thought of Glad, dying in her bed. I thought of my mom, lying on the sidewalk. I thought of Felix's red face. I thought of my frozen-in-a-block-of-ice dad. I thought of the secret smile that belonged to Dianne of the Flame-Red Hair.

A Tin Man wouldn't be afraid of a witch, especially if the circumstances were desperate.

So I said, "Yes."

Chapter 10

Back in the apartment, the cats meowed and traced figure eights around my ankles. My mom was still asleep. The air remained awkward.

"You can leave now," I told Felix.

"Are you sure?"

"I can take care of her. I'm almost eleven."

Felix nodded. "If you need anything—"

"You're just around the corner," I finished.

He scratched the top of each cat's head. "Good-bye, Miss Corwell."

"Bye, Mr. Farmer." I left off the *good* part because there was nothing *good* about the circumstances being so desperate that you were willing to put your life in the hands of a witch.

When Felix was gone, I pulled my mom's blanket

around her shoulders, then scooped up Neptune, who was crying at my feet. I turned on the light in Glad's room and sat in the chair.

"Mom was so *overwhelmed* that she had to lie down on the sidewalk," I told Bright Baby. "So Felix ordered a pizza. He helped make crowns, then we taught the boys to dance, and he appraised my ring." I paused. Bright Baby's eyes were closed; her thick lashes rested against her cheeks. "We were having a lot of fun until I told him I wished he was my dad. Then it all got ruined, just like everything else."

I reached out and touched one of Bright Baby's porcelain hands. "There's something I haven't told you because I didn't think you were old enough to understand. But I can't keep it a secret anymore. Mom is a terrible haircutter. She's running Glad's beauty parlor into the ground. Pretty soon there won't be a GLAD'S left."

I blinked, imagining GLAD'S going the way of the town Christmas tree, an empty space where once something bright and beautiful had stood. "There's a lot going on right now, Bright Baby. It's a lot to deal with, especially for the cats."

Neptune let out a tiny mew of affirmation.

"So I've asked somebody to help us *weather the storm*. Do you know what that means? It means life is so bad, if we don't do anything, we're going to get soaking wet. But this person, she's got umbrellas. She's got raincoats. Stuff like that. I hope." I took a deep breath. "The only worrisome part is—she might be a witch. I mean, she *is* a witch, if what Caleb says is true." I paused, waiting for my heart to stop fluttering, then continued: "Caleb said all witches are the same, but I don't know what that means. I don't know if she's good or bad. All I know is, if you come to life, Bright Baby, you'll be the best umbrella. If you were my sister, even if I were trapped in a hurricane, I'd never get wet."

Neptune let out another tiny mew. I kissed the top of his head. "And just so you know, I'd be a good big sister. I wouldn't hide my toys, or hang a KEEP OUT sign on my door, or tell you to stop being a copycat. I'd remember how lonely it was without you. I'd remember how it felt back when I was soaking wet."

I was quiet then as I slipped two fingers into Bright Baby's pocket.

But it was empty, so I left.

On Monday, at *The Place That Was and Always Would Be*, Raejean said, "I saw your mom passed out on the sidewalk."

We were at our lockers, at the back of the classroom. Raejean had a magnetic mirror hanging in hers. She liked to admire herself.

"She wasn't passed out," I said.

"*My* mom says she saw Felix Farmer at your apartment." She wriggled her eyebrows.

I put my face so close to hers that our noses bumped. "Stay out of my business, Raejean-Is-Mean. Go put your dog's tongue back in its mouth."

"Whatever you say, Beatrice-Feet-Kiss. You're just jealous I've got Montgomery, and all you've got is a bunch of ugly cats!"

"My cats aren't ugly," I hissed. Then the bell rang, so I had to sit down. I looked at all the heads in front of me. Not a single one had flame-red hair.

After Mrs. Hartley took attendance, I got out an *Ohio: The Heart of It All!* postcard. The steely-eyed cardinal looked nervous.

Dear D.,
There's a new boy at school who is both ridiculous and wily. I'm afraid that if you don't come soon he might try to lay claim to

the fossil. DON'T LET THIS HAPPEN! Come
to OHIO and get what's rightfully yours.
Love,
B.
P.S. I'm not joking about the boy. He has
porcupine hair.

I slipped the postcard into my desk. And then
the hours were *crunch, crunch, crunch*ed, *chew, chew,
chew*ed—until math class, when I got up to sharpen
my pencil. On my way back from the sharpener, as I
passed Caleb Chernavachin's desk, a small paper football fell at my feet. I picked it up. While Mrs. Hartley
talked about direct objects, I unfolded the paper.

grannee sez shell be yur witch. come after scool.

My heart quivered—part happy, part scared—but
I didn't pull a bead, because I was too busy imagining
Granny Witch in her long black dress.

The magic was coming. *Maybe.*

My wish was about to be granted. *Perhaps.*

All I needed was for Caleb Chernavachin to prove
that just this once he meant what he said.

Chapter 11

Caleb was waiting for me outside *The Place That Was and Always Would Be* when the bell rang. The cats were in a herd on the side of the building, and Caleb was trying to coax them over, but they just stayed where they were and hissed because I'd taught them to beware of strangers.

"Good afternoon, boys," I said. I was talking to the cats, but Caleb thought I meant him, too.

"Hey, Beatrice. You ready to meet my granny?"

I felt sort of ready. I wanted his wart-nosed granny's magic—if she had any—but I also felt scared and like asking a witch to cast a spell on the prettiest doll in the world might be a big mistake. So instead of answering, I crouched down in the grass and let the cats swish around me.

"What's wrong?" Caleb asked. "Cat got your tongue? Ha! *Get it?* You got cats all over you!"

"I'm quite aware of my current position." I stood up and brushed the fur off my clothes. *DO NOT,* said Glad's notes. Maybe what she was trying to tell me was, *DO NOT be afraid of Granny Witch.*

"Where do you live?" I asked.

"Water Street."

"Then let's go."

We walked. I didn't say much, but Caleb did enough talking for all of North America. First he told a story about how his mom was invited to meet the Queen of England. Her Majesty liked his mom so much that she gave her a corgi named Butterball. They brought the dog with them when they came to live with Caleb's granny.

"Wait," I interrupted. "Why did you and your mom come live with your granny?"

"My dad's doin' a wrestlin' tour, and my mom got real lonely, so we came to live with Granny. My mom's a movie star, but she's takin' a break to work at the garage door factory."

I rolled my eyes. So many lies. I could feel the possibility of Granny Witch slipping away.

"Anyway," Caleb said. "The whole reason I'm tellin' you this is because Butterball is missin'. So if you see a corgi waddlin' around with a Union Flag collar, that's my dog."

We had reached All That Is Amazing. I stopped and looked at Felix's flying bluebird. "Where are the posters?"

"What posters?"

"The missing posters," I said. "'Lost Dog,' that kind of stuff, you know."

Caleb pulled a freckled earlobe. "Granny's got no markers."

"You lie so much, you don't even know when you're lying."

"I know when I'm lyin', you crooked-haired cat-girl!" Caleb yelled, and then proceeded to tell another story that was even more ridiculous than the first.

"One time my dad was wrestlin' a bad guy named Jim the Giant Gem. Jim's whole body—his arms and legs and everything—were covered in diamonds, like they were glued on his skin."

"Why would he glue diamonds on his skin?"

"'Cause his name was Jim the Giant Gem," Caleb said. "Pay attention. So when my dad was wrestlin' him, the diamonds started fallin' off. Now, my dad's real smart. He knew those diamonds were worth a bunch of money, so he started scoopin' them up. But the problem was, he was wearin' his wrestlin' pants, and those don't have pockets, so he didn't have anywhere to put them. So guess what he did."

I considered for a moment where an imaginary wrestler without any pockets might put an imaginary handful of diamonds. "Did he throw them into the crowd?"

"No way!" Caleb crowed, eyes gleaming. "He's too smart for that. He swallowed them."

"Did he chew them up first?"

"Of course not. Then they wouldn't be worth nothin'. He swallowed them whole."

We'd reached the traffic circle. I could see the big purple GLAD'S sign. But Caleb still wasn't done with his story.

"Well, after the match was over, my dad had to go to the bathroom. So he sat on the toilet and—"

"Stop!" I cried, covering my ears. "This is disgusting!" I turned to the cats. "Don't listen, boys. Block your ears."

Caleb scowled. "I was just gettin' to the good part."

"I'm going to drop the cats off," I said to the ridiculous liar, and led my boys upstairs.

I checked the table for a letter from Dianne, then went to Glad's room, where I lifted Neptune from the bed. "I'm having some major doubts about the whole witch thing," I whispered to Bright Baby, "but

I'm going to see this through, just in case." Then I went to the kitchen and got two cheese sticks. Outside, I handed one to Caleb, who shoved the whole thing into his mouth.

He saw I was holding Neptune. "My granny's gonna want that cat."

I thought he was joking.

"I have to check in with my mom." I opened the door to the beauty parlor. Felix Farmer was in a styling chair, a purple cape draped across his shoulders. My mom stood behind him with her scissors.

"You've done an excellent job, as usual, Marta," Felix said to her reflection. He was so in love that you could practically see the hearts popping out of his eyes. That's the truth and a point-blank fact.

"Mom," I interrupted, "I'm going to meet Caleb Chernavachin's granny."

"Be home in time for dinner," she said.

"Hello, Neptune. Hello, Beatrice," said Felix.

"Hi," I said, trying to pretend I hadn't told him the embarrassing thing I'd told him Friday night. I turned back to my mom. "See you later."

"You still owe her for your haircut," I reminded Caleb on the sidewalk.

"I know. I got tons of money." He led us down the street.

Water Street started out nice, but then sort of crumbled. The houses got smaller, siding fell off, windows became cracked. We walked and walked, and then Caleb stopped in front of a bungalow whose paint had all chipped off. The steps leading up to the porch had collapsed. The yard was dirt, not grass.

"This is where my granny lives," Caleb said.

It wasn't what I'd imagined: no peaked roof, no gargoyles, no row of sleeping bats. "Are you sure you're telling the truth?" I asked.

"Honest." Caleb held up two freckled fingers that didn't look honest in the least.

I kissed the top of Neptune's head, then looked at the bungalow. It seemed kind of sad that a boy would live in a house as ramshackle as this one, but I knew a Tin Man wouldn't mind. A Tin Man wouldn't care if Granny Witch lived in a trash can. He'd figure out a way to get up on that porch, then step inside and say in his metallic voice, *Prove yourself, Witch! I need a spell to be cast.*

So I pulled a bead and said, "How do we get to the door?"

"Easy," said Caleb, and he ran and took a flying leap over the crumbled steps. He landed on the porch with a thud.

It looked pretty cool, so I did it, too.

"Meow," Neptune cried as we sailed through the air.

When we landed, Caleb gave me a high five, then opened the busted screen door.

The house was a mess. Trash covered the floor. There were holes in the wall and big spots in the floor where the carpet had been rubbed bare. On an old red couch, a woman sat, eating a bowl of chocolate ice cream. She had orange curly hair that puffed out from her head like a cloud, and yellow feathers dangled from her ears. She wore a purple tube top even though it was the middle of winter.

She glanced at us when we came in, then brought another spoonful of ice cream to her mouth.

"Is that your mom?" I whispered.

"Nah. My mom's asleep. She works the night shift," he whispered back.

"Then who is it?"

"Granny."

"You mean, *the witch*?"

Caleb nodded. "Yep."

I watched Granny Witch stir not a cauldron but a bowl of ice cream. No wart nose, no long black dress—never in my life had I seen a witch that looked like her. "You're lying."

"No, I ain't. Watch." He took a step toward the

couch. "Granny, this here's the girl who wants your help."

Granny Witch looked up from her bowl, then put another spoonful of ice cream in her mouth.

I cleared my throat. "My name's Beatrice," I said, because I'd read about the *art of conversation* in the encyclopedia.

"Caleb told me." Granny Witch's voice was deep and rumbly, like it was covered in dirt and hadn't been used in a hundred years.

Caleb just stood there, so I did, too. We watched her finish the bowl of ice cream, then lick the spoon.

"What's that you got?" she finally asked, looking at Neptune.

"A kitten." I held him up so she could see him.

"Ain't he cute." Granny Witch stood up. "Let me hold him."

Reluctantly, I handed him over. There was a pulse of panic in my heart.

Granny Witch pressed him against the bare skin above her tube top.

Neptune shrieked.

I tried to send him a thought message—*Don't worry; I won't let the orange-haired lady hurt you*—but thoughts couldn't travel inside the bungalow. There was something thick and wicked in the air.

"You want a sister, is that right?" Granny Witch asked.

I nodded.

"And you want me to make her for you?"

"If you can."

"Ha ha ha ha ha," Granny Witch cackled. "Of course I can." She pressed her lips to Neptune's head. His eyes bulged in horror. "But I don't work for free."

"I don't have any money," I said, and that was the truth and a point-blank fact. I'd thrown all my change into the fountain.

"You could pay with something else."

"Like what?"

She pursed her witchy lips and blew her witchy breath onto Neptune's back. He hissed, and she dangled him by the scruff of his neck. "This cat."

I gasped and snatched Neptune from her fingers. "Never."

She looked at me, feather earrings swaying. "You must not really want a sister."

I shook my head. I did want a sister. Oh, I did. Someone to play with while my mom was at work. Someone to snuggle up beside and whisper to under the covers. Someone to perch on my hip and sing to. The want was like a big wound in my chest. But I wouldn't sacrifice Neptune to heal it. I wouldn't turn that sweet kitten into a witch's pet. My eyes filled with tears. I mustn't cry. I mustn't. Tin Men rust if they get wet.

"Aw, come on, Granny. Not the cat. Pick somethin' different," Caleb pleaded.

Granny Witch put her hands on her hips. A smile spread across her face. "You want something different? How about this:

"Something borrowed, something blue.
She cut the line, and away it flew."

"What's that mean?" Caleb asked.

Granny Witch shrugged. "It's a riddle. Beatrice will have to solve it—*if* she wants a sister."

I was so angry then that I could spit. First she dangled my cat in the air, then she almost made me cry, and now she acted like Bright Baby wasn't the absolute hope of my heart. "I don't think you're a real witch," I blurted. "I think you're just a mean old granny who lives in a falling-down house."

"Not a real witch, huh?" She grabbed my wrist.

"Mark the spot,
Mark it dark,
Red as blood from the heart."

She rubbed her thumb across my wrist, back and forth. Her skin felt sharp as glass.

"Ow," I cried, yanking my arm away.

There, on my wrist, was a red circle with four lines sticking out, like a compass. "What did you do?" I gasped.

"Gave you a present," Granny Witch said, and then she laughed and laughed.

Chapter 12

You shouldn't have made her mad," said Caleb. "No good ever comes outta makin' Granny mad."

"She made me mad first." We were on the sidewalk and Caleb was holding Neptune so I could rub at the mark on my wrist. "It won't come off."

Caleb leaned over and looked. "Nope."

I spit on my wrist and rubbed some more. "Why won't it come off?"

"Like I told you: she's a witch."

"Well, I hate her." I snatched Neptune from his hands. "You have a horrible granny, Caleb Chernavachin."

He pulled an earlobe. "She's the only one I got."

I walked away then, faster than fast. I didn't run—that would look foolish—but I pretended I had rockets on my heels and blasted away. Caleb had to jog to keep up.

"Hey!" he called. "Beatrice. Hey! I'm sure it'll come off."

"When?" I asked, still blasting back to the beauty parlor.

"Three months?"

I stopped in the middle of the sidewalk. "You think I want to wear your granny's witch mark for three months?"

"No. Yes. I dunno. Tell you the truth, Beatrice, I don't know what you want. I thought you wanted Granny's help, but then you got in a fight with her instead."

I was so mad I wanted to scratch that boy's freckles off. "When I get my cats trained, you're the first person I'm going to have them attack." I turned back into a rocket and blasted away.

Caleb ran after me.

When I got to GLAD'S, I stopped. The beauty parlor was dark, which meant my mom was upstairs, making dinner.

"I sure am hungry," Caleb said.

I laughed. If that boy thought he was going to eat dinner with me after what Granny Witch had done . . . . I decided to say something, just for the pure meanness of it.

"If your parents are so rich, why don't they buy your granny something better than a shack to live in?"

Caleb stared at the dark beauty parlor windows. "They will. I'm gonna move real soon."

"A big mansion, huh?"

"That's right," he said, lifting his chin.

"I can't wait to see it."

"I doubt I'll invite you over."

Neither of us said anything then. It was one of those gloomy winter days where the sky is gray as a puddle. The kind of day that made you grumpy—whether Granny Witch had left her mark on you or not.

"Well, are you gonna solve her riddle?" Caleb finally asked.

I looked that ridiculous boy in the eye. "I wouldn't let your granny near Bright Baby if she were the last witch on Earth." Then I blasted up the staircase.

My mom was in the kitchen. "It's almost ready," she said.

I blasted by her, to Glad's room. The cats followed, crowding at my heels. I pulled out the desk chair and set Neptune on the bed.

"Hello, Bright Baby," I said, before noticing the boys were keeping an unusual distance. "What's wrong?"

It was Jupiter, the spotted fatty, who spoke up. "Meow."

Then I knew: they could smell the witch on me. And they were scared.

"I have something to show you," I said, because I believed in being honest. If I didn't teach them about the world, who would?

I stuck out my wrist. The room was quiet. I could feel their hesitation. And then Saturn the Brave, my wild-eyed tabby, stepped forward. Carefully, he licked the mark with his sandpaper tongue, and then it was like a spell was broken. The cats began to purr and rub against my legs. I scratched the tops of their heads, then turned my attention to Bright Baby.

"Well, she's real, and she's also bad, in case you were wondering. I hope she's not the third one. In the rule of three, I mean. First I found Neptune, then Caleb, but I don't think Granny Witch is number three. Another's coming, someone *good*. A genie, maybe. And *he'll* be the one who makes you come to life. I know it."

I paused and looked at her pocket. "Just like I know Glad's going to tell me something important." I closed my eyes because it's easier to send thoughts to faraway places when you aren't distracted. (I'd read about *focus* in the encyclopedia.)

DO NOT—DO NOT what, Glad?

I waited. I imagined Glad floating in the heavenly pool. I opened my eyes.

Bright Baby's eyes were open, her pocket no longer empty.

I pulled out the note, unfolded it, and read: *TRY*.

"*DO NOT TRY—? DO NOT TRY* to what?" I glanced at Venus, who sat on top of the dresser. "*DO NOT TRY* to solve Granny Witch's riddle? Well, you don't have to worry about that."

I scooped Neptune off the bed.

Thank you for another note, Glad, I said silently. Though a part of me didn't mean it. A part of me was getting annoyed with a message that came one word at a time. A part of me was worried I'd be twenty-five years old before the sentence was finished.

Pulling a bead, I left the room.

My mom was waiting at the table. She'd set out the salad spinner for Neptune, so I put him inside it, then took my own seat. The cats filled the empty chairs.

"Everything okay?" she asked.

She was good at reading faces. Even if you tried to make your face as uninteresting as a pancake, she'd find the tiniest trace of emotion to ask you about.

There was a drumstick on my plate and a clump of mushy rice shaped like a turtle. I hated drumsticks, and I hated mushy rice. "This looks disgusting," I said.

"What a disrespectful thing to say, Beatrice."

I smashed the turtle-shaped mushy rice with my fork. Now it looked like a jellyfish.

"What's on your wrist?" my mom asked.

"Oh, just an indelible mark that a witch branded me with."

"A *witch* drew that on you?"

"She didn't *draw* it. I don't know how she put it there. Caleb thinks it'll wear off in a few months, but I'm not so sure. I might be branded for life."

My mom reached across the table and touched my hand. "This is what I'm talking about, sweetie."

Neptune jumped out of the salad spinner and began to walk around our plates.

"I'm worried that you're living in a fantasy," my mom said.

"I *wish* Granny Witch were a fantasy."

"I'm not joking, Beatrice."

"Neither am I. I'll take you to meet her, if you want. But be warned: there aren't any steps leading up to her porch, and she eats a lot of ice cream."

My mom shook her head, then closed her eyes and started to do her breathing thing. Deep breath in . . . deep breath out . . . Finally, she said, "GLAD'S isn't earning enough money. I don't have any customers. I'm horrible at cutting hair."

"When I turn eighteen, I can be a stylist," I told her. "I'll be great. Customers will line the traffic circle, waiting to get in."

"You won't be eighteen for eight years."

"Time flies, Mom. It feels like I found Neptune yesterday, but really it was a month ago."

At the sound of his name, Neptune walked across the table and meowed in my face. My mom opened her eyes but didn't say anything.

"You can't close GLAD'S," I added. "This town will be destroyed without it."

"Let it be destroyed," my mom whispered.

I looked at the cats. They were as shocked as I was. "You're comfortable with destruction?"

"I'm not comfortable with anything right now." She took an *overwhelmed* breath.

"Well, in eight years you'll be fine. Eight short years, Mom. The blink of an eye."

She frowned. "You're making me worried again."

"No need to worry." I thought about telling her how Glad had said another word, so there were three now. Glad's important message was coming, like a leaky faucet, one slow drip at a time. But I didn't tell her. She'd say it was a fantasy—same as the witch mark.

I scooped an enormous forkful of rice and shoved it into my mouth.

My mom stared.

"Yes, ma'am," I told her, rice spilling from my lips. "No need to worry at all."

Chapter 13

I *was* **worried, though: about Bright Baby, about** *DO NOT TRY*, about the beauty parlor, and the witch mark. Oh, how I scrubbed that witch mark: with dish soap, laundry soap, shampoo, toothpaste— but it wouldn't come off, no matter what I used.

At *The Place That Was and Always Would Be*, I worried instead of listening to Mrs. Hartley. There weren't enough beads to pull for each worrisome thought that slinked through my head. To do that, I'd need a cord so long it stretched around the traffic circle. So when I ran out of beads, I made tally marks on the edge of my notebook. Then I got out a postcard, stared hard at that steely-eyed cardinal, and wrote to Dianne of the Flame-Red Hair:

Dear D.,

It's a trilobite, okay? I found a TRILOBITE. Can you believe it? I wanted it to be a surprise, but due to some unforeseen circumstances, I've decided to tip my hand. So, what do you think about that? Don't you want to see it? Well, hurry up and come back SOON!

Love,

B.

P.S. Please send a recipe for removing witch marks.

Another postcard said:

Dear D.,

Perhaps my last postcard wasn't clear. It's a whole entire trilobite. Not just a leg or an antenna. It's the whole FOSSILIFIC thing. I've never seen anything like it. Nor has anyone

else on the planet. Come on, Dianne, let me
show you this AMAZING discovery. OHIO is
where you belong!
Love,
B.
P.S. Would chewing on spearmint leaves do
the trick?

When I sharpened my pencil, Caleb flipped paper
footballs at my feet, but instead of picking them up, I
ground them with my heel. I was so mad at that boy
and his granny that I never wanted to read another of
his poorly spelled messages again.

Then one day, I was downtown after school. The
cats were at home because there was a chance of rain.
(They hated rain, and I hated how they smelled when
they got wet.) I had just been to the courthouse, since,
after the Granny Witch fiasco, I was back to square
one, trying to summon the magic of fountains. But
I was also on the lookout for Somebody Number
Three, the genie. As I scoured the square for mysterious lamps, that awful witch's words whirled through
my head:

Something borrowed, something blue.
She cut the line, and away it flew.

I wondered what that meant. I didn't *want* to wonder, but I did. I didn't *want* to hear Granny Witch's pebbly, dug-from-the-dirt voice chanting those witchy words, but I could.

Something borrowed, something blue.
She cut the line, and away it flew.

"Stop," I told my brain. "Please stop."

My brain wouldn't listen.

So I walked around, whispering the witch's words, until I found myself outside Cutie Pie Camera. I hadn't realized I was headed in that direction until there I was, watching a dad, mom, and baby blow bubbles at each other while Raejean's mom took their picture.

"Bubbles are stupid," I muttered.

"You know what else is stupid?" a voice asked.

I turned from the window. There stood Raejean, wearing a striped scarf and earmuffs. She held her pink purse. Montgomery's fluffy head and pink tongue stuck out the top.

"Hanging out with Caleb Chernavachin is what's stupid."

"I don't hang out with Caleb Chernavachin." I hadn't talked to him in a week, so that was the truth and a point-blank fact.

Raejean smiled in her fake way. "You know what *my* mom says? She says Caleb lives with a criminal."

That was probably the first interesting thing Raejean had ever said.

"You mean his granny or his mom?" I asked.

"Granny."

"I thought she was a witch, not a criminal."

"She's a *criminal* witch."

My heart did a double backflip in my chest. I'd never been in the company of a criminal before. I could have been arrested—I'd read about *accessory to crime* in the encyclopedia—which was both terrifying and exciting. I pulled a bead in my pocket.

"*My* mom says she moves from state to state so the police can't catch her. Before she moved here, she was a housekeeper in Kentucky. She stole thousands of dollars' worth of jewelry. Before that, she lived in Indiana, working at a gas station till she robbed it."

"How does your mom know this?" I asked.

Raejean tossed her curly hair. "She's a brilliant business owner."

"My mom's a business owner, too."

"For now," Raejean said.

I narrowed my eyes. "What's that mean?"

"You'll find out."

Oh, I didn't like Raejean saying that. *You'll find out*

meant *I know something you don't know.* And Raejean didn't know anything. *I* was the one who'd read the encyclopedia set. Raejean had probably never even read the back of a soup can.

"Take this!" I held up my wrist.

"What's that supposed to be? A spider?"

"Of course not. This is a powerful symbol, and now that I've shown it to you, it'll never leave your mind." I don't know why I said that. The words just rolled from my mouth, like boulders falling off a cliff. I flashed my wrist at Montgomery. "Now it's stuck in his mind, too."

"You're a weirdo," Raejean said. "You and Caleb Chernavachin belong together."

"You know where you belong? You belong in there"—I pointed at the Cutie Pie Camera window— "blowing bubbles with that stupid family."

It wasn't the best insult, but it's all I could think of.

"Goodbye, Beatrice-Feet-Kiss," Raejean said, turning toward the Cutie Pie Camera door.

"Raejean-Is-Mean!" I yelled, and blasted off down the sidewalk.

When I got to GLAD'S, I went to the entrance to say hi to my mom. But what I saw stopped me cold. There was a sign in the window, two feet tall, with black letters: FOR SALE. Under that it said:

Have you ever wanted to own a beauty parlor? Here's your chance. Long-established shop in search of a new owner. Comes with all supplies and equipment, plus a list of clients spanning nearly fifty years! See Marta for details.

I pulled the door open and stormed inside. The shop was empty except for my mom, who sat in a purple styling chair.

"Hello, sweetie," she said, as if the world was right and normal.

"What's that doing in the window?" I was so angry, I shook.

"I've agonized over this decision, Beatrice. I really have. It wasn't until Felix—"

"Felix?" I said.

"He made the sign for me."

"*Felix* made it?" Here, all this time, I'd thought Felix was a friend, a fellow cat lover. I'd wished he were my dad. But it turned out he was nothing but a backstabbing traitor. I wondered what Glad would think, if she knew the true identity of her favorite Downtown Business Council member.

"This is disappointing, Beatrice, I know, but it's for the best."

I looked at my mom in her *We're GLAD You're*

Here T-shirt, a shirt that, if she had her way, no one would ever wear again. "How dare you!" I cried. "How dare you say it's for the best when it's the absolute worst!"

I ran to the front of the beauty parlor and ripped the sign from the window.

My mom gasped as it fell to the floor in two pieces. "Beatrice Corwell!"

I was out the door before she could stop me. I ran, faster than fast, down the sidewalk, to Water Street. I ran till the houses got smaller and began to fall apart—and when I got to the dirt yard and the collapsed steps, I stopped.

Granny Witch's house was dark, but I thought I could see her shadow in there, and the cloudlike shape of her hair.

Something borrowed, something blue.
She cut the line, and away it flew.

I stared at the two dark windows.

My mom was going to sell GLAD'S. And when GLAD'S was gone, there would be absolutely nothing left.

Except Bright Baby.

She was all that remained, after Glad and her

beauty parlor, after my dad and Dianne. What I'm trying to say is, Bright Baby was the only physical thing left to hold on to. But she was enough. She had to be.

To hold a living, breathing sister in my arms—that wish, if I let it, could swell so big that it encompassed my whole hand. And maybe a genie could grant it, but I didn't have a genie.

What I had, right now, was a witch.

"Fine. You win," I said, staring at those dark windows. "I need Bright Baby. I need her desperately bad. I'm going to solve the riddle."

Chapter 14

On Valentine's Day, I let the cats wear their bows and gave them a saucer of cream with red food coloring. My mom left me a chocolate-covered marshmallow heart, which I ate, even though I was still to-the-moon upset with her. But some things are too precious to sacrifice—and a chocolate-covered marshmallow heart is one of them.

I didn't make a valentine for my mom, though. She had rehung the FOR SALE sign in the GLAD'S window. It looked horrible, all crumpled and taped together, and I hoped its shoddiness would deter potential buyers.

I did make a valentine for Bright Baby. I cut

different-colored squares out of tissue paper, then pasted them together in the shape of a heart. Before school, the cats and I gave it to her.

"Happy Valentine's Day, Bright Baby!" I taped the heart to the window. "See how it looks like stained glass when the sun shines through?"

Earth jumped onto the bed and nosed her body with his blue-gray head. "Meow."

I looked. He was right. I'd been so busy with Bright Baby's valentine that I hadn't noticed Glad sent one of her own. I pulled the note from the dress pocket.

"*TO*," I read.

The cats looked at me with quizzical expressions.

"Like the preposition *TO*," I clarified. "Not the number *TWO*. Or *TOO* as an adverb. Not: *There are TOO many cats in here.*"

They still looked confused. Mrs. Hartley would be so disappointed by their lack of grammar. "*DO NOT TRY TO—*" I said, putting all the words together. "*DO NOT TRY TO—*"

"Mew," Neptune cried in his tiny kitten voice. Which meant, *DO NOT TRY TO what?*

"Do not try to look so cute," I said, then scooped him up and set him on the bed.

I studied the tissue paper heart in the window, staring until it blurred. Then I sent Glad a message: *I wish you were here, and we could eat chocolate-covered marshmallow hearts together. But you're where you are, and I'm where I am. So I'll settle for the next word in your message.*

I touched Bright Baby's hand, then left the room. My mom was in the kitchen, drinking a cup of coffee. I picked up my backpack. "The cats and I are leaving," I told her, and then we did.

I was in no hurry to get to *The Place That Was and Always Would Be*, so we walked leisurely, looking in the shop windows. When we came to All That Is Amazing, I stopped. A surge of anger pushed through my chest, and I pulled a bead as hard as I could, practically crushing it in my fingers. How I hated Felix Farmer. I wished I had a slingshot so I could shoot his beloved bird right in the breast. Then I'd take my big metal foot—assuming I was a Tin Man—and crush it into a million shards of glass.

"What do you think, boys? Do you like the sound of that?"

"Meow," the cats said, which meant, *Yes, we'd love to sink our teeth into that glassy bird's flesh!*

We walked on, until we got to the bank of home-room windows. Then I entered *The Place* alone.

Seven hours to get through. Seven hours that felt like seven years. To pass the time, I imagined Dianne of the Flame-Red Hair, sketching trilobite-themed valentines in the desk beside me. Then I composed another postcard, trying to ignore the steely-eyed cardinal's angry stare:

Dear D.,

I'm going to be perfectly honest: You're really starting to get on my nerves. It's Valentine's Day, and where are you? Down in Florida, instead of where you should be: RIGHT HERE. I think I'm going to show someone else the trilobite. You've left me no choice. Blame yourself, best friend!

Love,

B.

P.S. Please send advice on disrupting the sale of historic buildings.

Postcard completed, I got out my notebook and found the page I'd labeled *How to Solve a Witch's Riddle.* I read the entries in the *Things You Can Borrow* column:

Library book
Cup of sugar
Dollar

I added three more:

Pencil
Jacket
Tissue

Next, I read the *Types of Lines* column:

Phone line
Clothesline
Zip line

And added:

Airline
Roofline
Skyline

The clock ticked. *Crunch, crunch, crunch, chew, chew, chew.* And finally, just before the bell rang, Mrs. Hartley said, "It's time to hand out carnations."

Everyone cheered—except me. I didn't care about carnations. I knew I wasn't going to get any.

Mrs. Hartley lifted a five-gallon bucket filled with flowers from behind her desk.

"Ooh," everyone cried.

Except me. I said, "Flowers die," which is the truth and a point-blank fact, but no one paid any attention.

The carnations were red for love, pink for friendship, and yellow for hope. You could order them at lunch to send to your friends. Since *my* one and only friend, She of the Flame-Red Hair, was in Florida, I didn't order one. But lots of other people did. (I'd read about *herd behavior* in the encyclopedia.)

Mrs. Hartley picked a red carnation from the bucket and read the tag on its stem. "Raejean."

Raejean bounced to the front of the room. She wore a pink sweater and dangly heart earrings. She grabbed her carnation and smiled her big, fake smile. "Thank you so much," she said, then sat back down.

Mrs. Hartley picked out another carnation. "Raejean."

Raejean went up, got her carnation, said "Thank you so much," and sat back down.

Mrs. Hartley lifted a third flower. "Raejean."

That's when I pinched my arm. Sometimes, you think you're awake, but you're actually stuck in a horrible dream. I thought maybe, if I pinched myself, Raejean would disappear. But no: I wasn't *dreaming* Raejean was receiving all the carnations. She really was.

Jessica got one. Jen got two. The class laughed when Brad, a boy, had his name called. But every other carnation went to Raejean. Her fists were so full of stems that she could barely hold them.

Then there was one carnation left, a yellow one, for hope. Mrs. Hartley picked it up. I crossed my fingers. I hoped I'd get the hope carnation, even though flowers die, even though a true and proper Tin Man would have no desire for something as useless as a flower.

"Beatrice," Mrs. Hartley said.

Raejean gasped.

I went up and got my carnation, then strode back to my desk. My fingers trembled as I lifted the tag on the stem and read, in a familiar, poorly spelled hand:

I hope u will let me help u solv my grannee's riddl

I looked up. Caleb turned around in his desk.

"Thank you," I mouthed.

"No problem," he mouthed back.

Then the final bell finally rang, and I walked out of class with my head held high because I was a girl with a flower.

Chapter 15

Caleb was waiting outside with the cats.

"That's one pretty petunia," he said.

"It's a carnation," I corrected him.

"Same difference. A flower's a flower." He tugged his earlobe. "So?"

I imagined Granny Witch, eagerly leaning over her crystal ball, waiting for my answer. "I want you to help me solve the riddle."

"Hot dog!" Caleb slapped his hands together. "Let me think how it goes." He squinted, trying to remember. *"Somethin' old and blue, on the fence it grew."*

"That sounds like *mold*, Caleb. She doesn't want *mold*. It's this:

"Something borrowed, something blue.
She cut the line, and away it flew."

Caleb scowled. "I hate riddles."

"Let's think of things that are blue," I suggested. So that's what we did as we walked home. "Blueberries," I began.

"Leprechauns," Caleb said.

I looked at him. "Leprechauns aren't blue."

"Some are."

Leprechauns aren't blue. That's the truth and a point-blank fact. But I didn't feel like fighting about it. "Fine. Leprechauns."

"The sky," Caleb said.

"The ocean."

We'd reached the downtown. I gazed in the store windows as we passed. And then I saw something that made me stop.

"Wait."

We were in front of All That Is Amazing. Felix's glass bluebird hung, as always, from its fishing line in the window. My heart tap-danced in my chest.

"Has your granny ever been downtown?"

"Of course."

"Has she ever been in Felix Farmer's store?"

"Nah. But she looked in the window. Said she bet

that bird was worth a whole bunch of money, but she could trick the owner into sellin' it to her dirt cheap."

I looked at Felix's bird, and I thought a lot of thoughts: about *overwhelmed* moms and frozen dads, dead grandmas and runaway best friends. I thought of words that came so slowly, one drip . . . drip . . . drip at a time. I thought of FOR SALE signs and being betrayed by someone you trusted.

Finally, I said to Caleb, "Do you know how to create a distraction?"

"Yeah."

"When I give the signal, you distract Felix, and I'll steal the bird."

"Why are you stealin' the bird?"

"To solve the riddle," I said.

"Oh, man!" Caleb cried. "Oh, man!"

I couldn't tell if he was scared or excited. "Ready?"

He licked his lips. "Ready. But wait a second: I thought Felix was your friend."

"Not anymore." I opened the shop door.

"Mercury, Venus, Earth, Mars, Jupiter, Saturn, Uranus, Beatrice, and Caleb—so good to see you," Felix said from behind the counter, where he was polishing vases. "How was school?"

"Fine," I said.

He spotted my carnation. "Nice flower."

"It's a petunia," Caleb boasted. "I gave it to her."

Felix raised an eyebrow.

I shrugged.

"So, what can I help you two with today?"

"Tweet, tweet," I said. I'd decided a bird chirp would be the signal to distract Felix. The problem was, I'd forgotten to tell Caleb, so when I tweeted, he just stared.

I tried again. *"Tweet, tweet."*

"Pardon?" Felix asked.

And now the cats, who'd jumped up on the counter, looked at me, too. I turned to Caleb and screamed with my eyes: *Tweet is the signal!*

"Oh," he said. "Oh!" Then he said to Felix, "You wanna see a really cool wrestlin' move?"

Felix cocked his head. "Sure."

"You gotta come to the back of the store, then close your eyes 'cause it's a surprise."

"Odd request—and yet somewhat intriguing," Felix said as Caleb led him away.

I set my carnation on the counter, then hurried to the display window and climbed inside. I reached for the bluebird, then happened to glance back.

The cats sat in a row, watching me.

"Meow," said Uranus, the white runt. Though prone

to jealousy, he was also the most honest and thus deeply disturbed by my plan.

"Felix *betrayed* us. He's trying to help Mom sell GLAD'S," I said. "Besides, this is for Bright Baby. I'm doing this for her."

Cats don't cry, of course, but Uranus's face filled with sorrow. He lowered his head.

I didn't care. It was a very Tin Man–type moment. I felt nothing, not worry, nor fear, nor guilt, as I took hold of the fishing line. I gave it one hard tug—and *snap!* The line broke. The bird was in my hand.

I looked at it, its smooth blue body and the ruby heart in its chest.

The mark on my wrist burned like fire as a witch's cackle rattled in my ears.

Chapter 16

The cats stared at me with scornful eyes.

"Shh," I told them, then opened the shop door. One by one, they leapt from the counter and swished outside.

Raejean stood on the sidewalk.

Quickly, I hid the bluebird behind my back.

"What's that?" Raejean had her bouquet of carnations in one hand, the pink purse with Montgomery in the other.

"Nothing," I said.

"You can't hide *nothing*."

"Who said I'm hiding something?"

"It's called body language," she said.

"I thought it was called *mind your own business*."

"You're just jealous I got all these flowers." Raejean

brought the bouquet to her nose and took a big, fake whiff. Montgomery's tongue quivered.

Caleb stepped out of All That Is Amazing then. "You got it?" he asked.

"Got what?" said Raejean suspiciously.

"Nothing," I told her. Then to Caleb I said, "Yes."

"Good. Let's get outta here."

"Goodbye, Raejean-Is-Mean. I hope your flowers don't die," I said as we walked away.

"Beatrice and Caleb sitting in a tree!" she yelled after us.

We pretended not to hear her, all except Earth, who turned around and hissed.

"Did Felix suspect anything?" I asked Caleb as we headed toward the traffic circle.

"Nah. He was too busy rubbin' his neck from the headlock I put him in." Caleb stuck out his palm. "Let me see it."

I placed the bird in his hand.

He looked it over for a few seconds, then gave it back. "Of all the things in the world, I don't know why Granny would want that."

"I do," I said. The bird was both beautiful and rare. Even a mean, ice-cream-eating witch couldn't help but desire it.

We came to GLAD'S, and I purposefully looked

the other way so as not to see the poster in the window.

But Caleb said, "Hey, your beauty parlor's for sale."

"No, it's not."

"Yeah, it is. There's a sign."

"Signs are meaningless—especially signs made by Felix Farmer."

I could feel Caleb's stare. "You sure are actin' weird."

"Maybe the witch mark has entered my bloodstream." (I'd read about *viremia* in the encyclopedia.)

Caleb pulled his ear. "I guess."

We kept walking, turning on Water Street and passing the falling-down houses. When we got to Granny Witch's, we stopped. The cats meowed anxiously.

"It'll be okay. There's nothing to worry about," I said, but the Tin Man feeling was gone. Instead of smooth metal, now my heart was bumpy as a toad—and most of the bumps were fear.

"Is your mom home?" I asked, thinking maybe, if we got into trouble, she could help.

Caleb shook his head. "Her shift already started."

So we ran, without backup, across the dirt yard and leapt over the collapsed steps. We landed with double thumps on the porch.

"Granny," Caleb called, pushing open the screen door, "Beatrice got somethin' for you."

Granny Witch was on the couch again, eating ice cream and watching a judge show. A crystal ball was beside her. "What is it?" she asked, not taking her eyes off the TV.

"The thing you asked for. In the riddle," said Caleb.

"Hold on. I want to hear the verdict."

So we held on. We watched Granny Witch watch the judge show. Peacock feathers were in her ears. She had on her tube top, but over it was a big brown fur coat. She looked like a bear.

I glanced at the bluebird in my hand. It seemed different here than at Felix's. At All That Is Amazing, I could imagine the bird flying, its tiny heart burning like a bright red coal, but here it was just a dust-covered knickknack.

"Fool!" Granny Witch yelled at the judge because she didn't like the ruling. Then she turned off the TV and said to me, "Bring it here."

Slowly, I approached, handed her the bird, then took a giant step back.

Granny Witch laughed. Her cackle filled the house, reverberating off the walls. Then abruptly it stopped. She looked at me, and I remembered what Raejean had said, about her being a criminal, and I knew right then it was true. Every wicked deed she'd done was a cold glint in her eyes.

"Get my robe," she told Caleb.

He left the room, then returned with a satin bathrobe. Granny Witch took the belt from the waist and looped it around the bluebird's neck. Then she climbed up on the coffee table and tied the bird to the light bulb on the ceiling.

"That bird looks dead, Granny," Caleb said.

Granny Witch laughed.

But Caleb was right. Felix's beloved bird was dead, and I was the one who'd killed it. I looked away, my stomach full of sickness, toward a window that was all gray smudges. I pulled a bead in my pocket.

"Will you help her now?" Caleb asked.

"Guess I have to."

"When?" I asked.

"When it's time." She plopped back down on the couch and wrapped her bear fur all around her so the only human part showing was her head. Then she stared straight ahead, unmoving.

Minutes passed. Finally, I whispered to Caleb, "What's she doing?"

"Takin' her nap."

"With her eyes open?"

"Yep."

"When's she going to help me?"

Caleb pulled his earlobe. "I don't know. Not now."

"Well, that's some witch you got there."

"Things used to be different," said Caleb sadly.

I nodded because I knew what he meant. Things used to be different for me, too.

"I've got to go," I said. And then, to cheer him up: "Thanks again for the carnation."

"At least Raejean didn't get all of 'em."

I hopped off the porch and ran to the cats. They were curious to know what had happened, but I didn't want to give them nightmares, so I just said, "She accepted my offer, which means my wish will soon be granted."

They were skeptical, I could tell, but didn't press me. So we headed home, Felix's dead bird dangling like one of Mrs. Hartley's misplaced modifiers in my mind.

That night, I put on my Glad ring, the one shaped like a flower. I don't know why. Maybe I was feeling poor, and the five-thousand-dollar ring made me feel rich. Maybe I wanted to look at something pretty, after the ugliness of Granny Witch's house. Either way, I put on the ring and sat with Bright Baby. I didn't check her pocket, because I knew Glad wouldn't leave two words for me on the same day.

"Granny Witch is going to help us," I told Bright Baby, "but I don't know when, so we have to hang on till she gets here."

And then I started to cry, but the tears were on the inside, and since my eyes were locked tight, they couldn't spill out. Tin Men don't cry, though, even on the inside, so I had to pull a bead. And then I pulled another, for Glad, and one for Dianne and my mom. There was a bead for Neptune, who was growing up too fast, and two for Felix: one for betraying me and one for my betraying him. And last of all, I pulled a bead for my dad in Antarctica. So many beads, so many bumps. Sometimes it seemed I'd never make my heart all shiny and flat.

I tried, though. I sat with Bright Baby, pulling bead after bead, and when I ran out, I started all over again.

I pulled till my fingers became so tired that I dropped the cord. Then I fell asleep in the chair.

I decided to walk alone to *The Place That Was and Always Would Be* the next morning. A lot had happened—a lot was about to happen—and I needed space to mentally prepare.

"Not today, my sweets," I told the boys when they lined up to escort me. "Today I must venture out on my own."

My stomach was a sea of worry as I walked downtown. "The display window is the eye of the store," Felix had told me. And now All That Is Amazing had an eye that was missing its iris.

The fishing line was still there. Felix had left it hanging, empty. Under the fishing line was a crystal vase. Inside the vase was a yellow carnation, the one I had accidentally left on the counter.

It was enough to break your heart: the empty line, the forgotten carnation. *If,* that is, your heart was a muscle and not a shiny piece of metal. And *if* a witch wasn't about to make your tip-top secret wish come true.

Chapter 17

I know what you did," Raejean said.

We were hanging our backpacks in our lockers. Her curly hair was tied up with a pink ribbon, and two locks coiled snakelike down the sides of her face.

"No, you don't."

"Yes, I do." She leaned in so close I could smell her bubble gum lip gloss.

"You're a big bluffing bluffer," I said, even though I wasn't sure that was true.

"Where's your carnation?"

"In a vase."

"Exactly," she said triumphantly, as if she'd gotten me to admit something significant, even though flowers sit in vases all over the world. That's the truth and a point-blank fact.

The bell rang, and Raejean went to her desk, bumping into me on purpose.

At my desk, as Mrs. Hartley underlined prepositional phrases on the board, I thought every mean thought I could think at the back of Raejean's head. And then I imagined every mean thought Dianne of the Flame-Red Hair would've had, if her desk was still beside me. When I was all out of thoughts, I pulled out a postcard. The steely-eyed cardinal looked worried today.

Dear D.,
I'm running out of postcards, and I wonder if you even care. The OLD Dianne in OHIO would've cared, but I'm beginning to think the NEW Dianne in FLORIDA couldn't care less. I think the NEW Dianne doesn't like trilobites or anything, really, except palm trees and sand. If I'm wrong about this—and I sincerely hope I am—PROVE IT!
　　　　　　　　Love,
　　　　　　　　B.
P.S. Remember the bluebird that hung in the

All That Is Amazing window? Well, it's gone now, just like you.

I returned the postcard to my desk and focused on the witch mark, massaging it with my thumb. Next, I got out my gerbil eraser and rubbed until nothing was left of the rubber animal except a little pink nub. But the witch mark still hadn't faded one bit.

"Come on, Granny Witch," I whispered, imagining her asleep in her fur coat, eyes wide open, like a hibernating bear. "It's time to grant my wish."

My mom invited Felix to dinner. She didn't tell me beforehand.

"Could you get that for me?" she asked when there was a knock at the door.

The last person I expected to see was the bald-headed traitor, holding a pointy loaf of bread.

"Good evening," he said.

"Evening," I replied, because no evening with Felix present could be described as good.

"I'm so happy you could join us." My mom set a casserole on the table.

"Marta, I wouldn't miss eating casserole with you for all the tea in China." Felix laughed, to make it sound like a joke, as the hearts popped out of his eyes.

The cats joined us at the table. Some had to sit three to a chair. Once we were all served, Felix said, "Beatrice, did you ever show your mom what we taught them to do?"

I took a nibble of casserole and shrugged, as if teaching eight cats to perform a choreographed number wasn't worth mentioning.

"What did you teach them?" my mom asked.

"You didn't tell her?" said Felix.

I looked at the cats and shrugged again. "I must have forgotten." If Felix thought he was allowed to make FOR SALE signs for dead grandmas' beauty parlors just because he'd taught their granddaughters' cats to dance—well, he needed to do some better thinking. (I'd read about *faulty logic* in the encyclopedia.)

The faithless Farmer changed the subject then, and he and my mom spent the rest of the meal discussing boring adult topics. I watched him carefully, trying to detect anything that suggested he knew I was the one who'd taken his bluebird. He didn't seem suspicious, but once, in the middle of a discussion, he said loudly, "I know what it's like to lose an object of great sentimental value." Then he and my mom both looked at me, but I pretended not to notice.

After dinner, we played Old Maid. I didn't want to play Old Maid with the *Traitor of Downtown*, but my mom made me. So as Felix shuffled the deck, I hoped with every cell in my body he'd get stuck with the Old Maid card. The cats hoped, too, because they were loyal, which meant our enemies were one and the same.

The problem with playing cards with Felix was that he was fun to play cards with. He moaned and groaned at a bad draw and cheered and thumped his elbows on the table at a good one. All of which made it easy to forget what I had done to him and what he had done to me. In fact, Felix's shenanigans made me start thinking different thoughts entirely.

Like how, if we were at Cutie Pie Camera, Rae-jean's mom would take our picture. And she'd tell each of us to hold up our cards. She'd tell my mom to smile at Felix, and Felix to smile at my mom, and she'd have me seated between them, grinning at the camera. So if a girl was walking down the sidewalk and decided to press her nose to the window, she'd see a woman, a man, and a girl with crooked hair, who she'd think was their daughter.

And the girl would say to herself, *Look at that family in there, pretending to be happy. What a bunch of fakers.* But deep in her heart, in a tiny little spot she couldn't make not feel, no matter how hard she tried, she'd whisper, *How I wish I were one of them.*

Every day, I walked by All That Is Amazing on my way to *The Place That Was and Always Would Be.* Every day, I looked in the window and saw the empty fishing line, the vase with the yellow carnation. Every day, the carnation lost a bit more color; the petals became brown and dry.

Still, Felix let it sit there.

"When is that no-good granny of yours going to help me?" I asked Caleb after school.

He shrugged. "Beats me."

"I stole the bird. She *has* to help me. She *promised.*"

"I keep tryin' to tell you, Beatrice. You can't make Granny do nothin'. You just gotta wait for the mood to strike her. Don't worry. She'll do it when she's ready."

But I did worry. I still had a whole handful of

wishes. Not a finger had been freed. So I pulled beads, I found pennies on the sidewalk to throw in the fountain, and I worked on my postcards:

Dear D.,
Remember that ridiculous boy I told you about, the one with the porcupine hair? I showed him the trilobite. What do you think about that? Are you sad? Well, don't worry. I just showed him a little part. One of the legs, is all. You'll be the first to see the whole thing. All you've got to do is get here FASTER THAN FAST!

Love,
B.

P.S. Sometimes I dream I'm back in the creek, catching crawdads with you, and it's so real that when I wake up, I can feel the mud between my toes.

Then one day, finally, Caleb flicked a paper football on my way back from the pencil sharpener. At my desk, I read:

I gasped.

"Is something wrong, Beatrice?" Mrs. Hartley asked.

"I do apologize, but I just received a piece of life-altering information."

"Is that right?" She raised an eyebrow. "And where did this life-altering information come from? Was it telepathy from the man on the moon?"

The class laughed. Raejean laughed the fakest.

"I can't provide specifics," I said.

"Go stand in the corner. Right there."

It was a baby punishment. Mrs. Hartley knew it, which is why she chose it, to embarrass me. But I, with eight cats, a crooked haircut, and a mom who did deep-breathing techniques on the sidewalk, was not easily embarrassed. True Tin Man–style, I didn't care that I'd been made a spectacle. I stood in the corner and imagined Bright Baby come to life, trying to steal Old Maid cards from my hand.

When the bell rang, I expected Caleb to be waiting for me, but he wasn't. The cats and I walked home alone. I checked the kitchen table for a letter.

Then, inside Glad's room, I told Bright Baby the news.

"The witch is coming, but don't be scared. Now I think she's a good witch."

Uranus the Honest meowed.

"Well, she's not *exactly* good, but I don't think she's bad, either."

Now it was Jupiter's turn to correct me. He jumped on my lap and nudged the mark on my wrist.

"Fine," I said. "I know she's bad. She might be *really, really* bad. But she's the only witch we have, and I already stole the bird, so I might as well let her help us. There. What do you all think of that?" I said the last part to the cats. They could tell they were getting on my nerves, so they bit their tongues and silently swished their tails.

"All I'm trying to say is, don't worry, Bright Baby." I touched her porcelain hand. "Everything's going to be okay."

Then I closed my eyes and sent a thought to Glad. *Another word, please? If you're not too busy. If your hands aren't wet from the pool.*

I counted to ten slowly, and then I checked the pocket. A note!

The cats meowed, curious.

"MAKE," I read. "DO NOT TRY TO MAKE—"

What? DO NOT TRY TO MAKE what? A deal with Granny Witch? Well, it's too late, Glad, for that.

I picked up Neptune, and we all headed down to the beauty parlor.

Samantha, the owner of Panis-Panis bakery, was talking to my mom. She had on her white baking outfit and wore her hair in a braid spanning the length of her back. Elmer, her Doberman pinscher, sat at her feet. When Samantha came in to get her braid trimmed, she always brought Elmer, too. No one could make his coat shine like my mom could.

"Hey, Beatrice," Sam said.

"Hey."

"I'm trying to help your mom think of potential buyers for the beauty parlor."

My mom picked up a broom and began to sweep the floor of nonexistent hair.

"We don't want your help," I said.

"Beatrice!" my mom cried. Then she lowered her voice and said to Samantha, "Call me. We'll talk later."

Samantha nodded. "See you, Beatrice. See you, kitties."

All nine of us ignored her. When she and Elmer

were gone, I said, "You can't sell GLAD'S. I won't let you."

My mom stopped sweeping. "*I'm* the one in charge here." She pointed the broom handle in my face.

Oh, that made me mad. I hated having things pointed at me, especially broom handles. I turned toward the FOR SALE sign. My plan was to rip it into so many pieces that no tape could save it.

"Don't you dare!" my mom yelled, because not only was she good at reading faces; she was also good at reading hands.

My fingers brushed the poster board.

And then, right at that moment, Caleb and Granny Witch walked in.

Chapter 18

"**M**ay I help you?" my mom asked. "Are you here for a haircut?"

Granny Witch cackled and shook her head. Big black crow feathers swung from her ears. She held a small red case in her hand. "I do my own hair," she said in her pebbly, bottom-of-a-creek-bed voice.

"They're here to see me," I interjected. "That's Caleb Chernavachin." I pointed him out, in case my mom didn't recognize him.

"Hello, Caleb," she said, but her eyes stayed focused on Granny Witch.

"Caleb and I are working on a project. His granny is going to help us."

Granny Witch smiled. Her incisors looked sharp.

"What kind of project?" my mom asked.

I didn't dare tell her that I'd made a contract with a witch, so I called the cats instead. *"Here, kitty-kitty-kitty."*

The boys appeared from their hiding spots. Fur bristled, they gathered at my feet—all except Mercury, who walked up to Granny Witch and hissed.

"That cat looks mean," said Caleb.

"Don't be ridiculous," I said. "Mercury's not mean. He's just protective."

Granny Witch eyed Neptune. "Let me hold that kitten."

"No way." I turned to my mom. "We're going to go work on the project now."

"Hmm," she said, which was not a good sign.

"Come on, boys." I quickly led the cats to the door, hoping Caleb and Granny Witch would follow. They did.

"Where's the doll?" Granny Witch asked as soon as we entered the apartment.

"I'll show you." I led her to Glad's room.

There Bright Baby was, in her white lace dress. Granny Witch moved the desk chair beside the bed.

"I don't have a lot of time." She set the red case on her lap and closed her eyes.

The cats jumped up on the dresser and sat tall and straight, like gargoyles.

Don't worry, I told them with my eyes. *Nothing bad is going to happen.*

We don't believe you, their eyes said back.

Granny Witch let out a long sigh.

"What's she doing?" I whispered to Caleb.

"Maybe callin' some spirits or somethin'."

"No talking!" Granny Witch ordered. Then she said, "This doll is not alive."

Which was a very obvious and time-wasting thing to say, especially for someone who was supposedly in a hurry. "That's why I asked you to come," I reminded her.

"Shut up!" she yelled.

The cats hissed.

"This doll would like to come to life," Granny Witch continued. "And she will—with the help of this." She opened the red case. Inside was a dead toad. Brown and flat, it appeared to have been run over by a truck and then set out in the sun to dry, like a raisin.

Granny Witch put the dead toad in the middle of Bright Baby's chest. Then she closed her eyes again and chanted:

"Come to the living place.
There's a girl who desires your face.
When you are born—
She'll no longer be torn.
Come now and run the race."

Then she turned to me and said, "Tell me what you want."

"I want Bright Baby to come to life."

"What else?"

"I want my mom not to sell GLAD'S."

"More!" Granny Witch demanded.

"I want Dianne to move back to Ohio."

"More!"

The cats growled, the sound low and rumbly in their throats.

"Um . . ." It's hard to voice all the wishes hovering on your fingers when a witch puts you on the spot.

"I know what *I* want: a Corvette," Caleb said.

"Shut up!" Granny Witch ordered. "More," she said to me.

"I want to turn into a Tin Man," I whispered.

Caleb wrinkled his nose. "What's a Tin Man?"

"If you say another word . . . ," Granny Witch snarled at him.

"That's all," I said.

She shook her head. The black feathers dangled. "No, it's not."

I looked at the cats in their gargoyle poses. *Tell her no more*, their eyes begged.

I looked at the toad, all brown and flat on Bright Baby's dress. I wondered if the toad itself was magic, or if the magic came from the words Granny Witch said. Then I stopped wondering and opened my mouth. Out came a sentence I hadn't planned: "I want my dad to come back."

Granny Witch snapped her fingers. "That's it," she hissed.

"No!" I cried, not knowing what I'd done, just knowing, somehow, it was a mistake. "I take it back!"

"You can't take it back."

"But I didn't mean it! That's not one of my resolutions! I don't want my dad to come back. I want him to stay in Antarctica with the penguins."

"I want *my* dad to come back," Caleb mumbled.

With outstretched arms, Granny Witch chanted:

"The girl has spoken.
She's made her choice.
Now the world
Shall heed her voice."

She bent down over Bright Baby and said: "Arise."

There was a hissing, crackling sound. Then everything was still. Bright Baby lay in Glad's bed, unmoving. The apartment was silent.

"Is she alive?" I finally asked.

"Yep." Granny Witch picked up the toad and put it back in the case.

I observed Bright Baby's pale, porcelain skin. "She doesn't look alive."

"Neither do I." Granny Witch flashed her sharp teeth and cackled.

The cats hissed as worry swirled inside my stomach. I pulled a bead.

Then there was a knock at the door, more like a pounding. Three big strikes. *Bang! Bang! Bang!*

Granny Witch froze.

Caleb pulled his ear.

Neptune let out a tiny kitten mew that meant, *I'm scared*.

But I wasn't scared. I knew what those three bangs meant. The third someone, the *good* someone—the genie—had, at long last, arrived.

I picked up Neptune and went to the door.

Santa stood on the stairs. "Ho, ho, ho," he said.

Chapter 19

Santa was missing a few things: the long white beard, the roly-poly belly, the reindeer, the sled, the sack of toys. But it was definitely him on the top stair, wearing a red velvet suit and a grin.

"Don't you recognize me?" he asked.

"I recognize you." Santa suits are quite distinctive.

"It's been a while, huh?"

I wasn't sure what he meant. It was the end of February. I'd last seen a Santa at the mall in December. That was two months ago, which seemed less than *a while*. But maybe time was measured differently at the North Pole.

"How about a hug?" Santa stretched out his arms.

"No." I did not hug strangers. I especially did not

hug strangers in Santa suits. (I'd read about *kidnapping* in the encyclopedia.)

"Aw, come on," he said, and before I could slam the door, he stepped into the apartment.

A Tin Man would have swung his axe and cut that red suit right in two. But I was still a girl. I didn't have an axe, just a cord of beads in my pocket. So I used the only weapon I had: my voice.

I screamed—really loud.

Caleb came running. So did Granny Witch. The cats, too.

Santa was undeterred. "Come here, honey," he cooed, arms outstretched like Frankenstein's monster.

I pressed Neptune to my chest—and that's when I remembered. I *did* have a physical weapon. It had seven sets of pointy teeth and sharp claws.

"Sic him, boys!" I cried.

My boys did. First there was a rumble in their throats, and then they leapt, fur flying, through the air. They landed on Santa: one on each arm, two on each leg, with Mars clinging to his stomach.

"What are you doing?" Santa cried as he stumbled around, trying to shake loose the cats.

"Look at that," said Granny Witch.

"It's like a cartoon," Caleb marveled.

"Bea-Bea, it's me!" Santa yelled as he flailed about.

My heart, at the sound of those words, swelled. There was only one person in the world who called me Bea-Bea. And it wasn't Santa.

"Dad?"

My dad turned. Now his arms were stretched out straight at his sides. He looked like a scarecrow that had been attacked by a pack of feral cats. "The one and only."

Caleb gave a long, low whistle.

"I'll be," Granny Witch said.

I, however, was silent. All I could think was, *My dad is the third somebody. My dad has completed the rule of three.*

"Could you get your cats off me, Bea-Bea?" my dad asked, shaking his arms. The cats bobbed up and down.

"Sure," I said—then realized I had a problem. Though I had taught the cats to attack, I hadn't taught them how to *unattack*, which meant I didn't know how to get them off.

"Okay, boys. Time to stop," I tried.

The cats stayed attached.

"That's my dad. He won't hurt me."

The cats remained in place. It had been so long since they'd seen my dad, they'd probably forgotten what a "dad" even was. Cats aren't elephants. No matter what felines claim, their memories are far from perfect.

And then I thought of one last thing I could say: the irresistible cry. *"Here, kitty-kitty-kitty."*

Seven jaws released. Fourteen sets of claws retracted. Seven thumps later, my boys were on the floor.

My dad's Santa suit looked like it had gone through a paper shredder.

"Sorry about your outfit," I said.

He smiled and stuck out his arms. "Now can I get that hug, Bea-Bea?"

I set Neptune on the floor and walked toward him. A second later, velvet fabric was against my nose.

"I sure missed you," he said.

My ear was pressed to his chest, so his voice sounded far away, like it was coming from inside a tunnel. Or maybe a block of ice.

"I missed you, too," I said, hugging my dad tighter than tight as all the thoughts in the universe spun, tornado-like, in my head.

I closed my eyes to stop them. I didn't want to think about Caleb standing there, or Granny Witch and her dead toad. I didn't want to think about Bright Baby, who still had porcelain skin, which meant

Granny Witch had freed up the wrong finger. She'd granted *a* wish but not *the* wish for which I'd paid her. Which meant I had a problem. I'd been given my dad, but not my sister. And no genie was coming to make it right.

Chapter 20

I hugged my dad for so long that when I finally stopped hugging him, Caleb and Granny Witch had left. I decided to show him around the apartment.

"You must want to be an astronaut," he said when he saw all the space-themed objects in my room.

"That's for the cats."

Warily, he eyed the boys, who slinked behind him.

When your dad comes to visit after a two-year absence, you want to impress him. Even if his arrival means the wrong wish was granted, you still want to show him something that will make him think it was worth leaving the penguins.

I had only one such object. I opened the jewelry box on my dresser, took out Glad's flower ring, and placed it in his palm.

"Where'd you get this?"

"Glad." As soon as I spoke her name, I remembered that I hadn't seen my dad since I was eight, which meant he didn't know Glad was gone. "She died."

"No."

I nodded, then waited for him to say something else, like, *What happened?* Or, *I'm sorry to hear that.*

But he didn't say either of those things, so I said, "Felix says it's worth five thousand dollars."

"Who's Felix?"

"A big, bald-headed betrayer." I took the ring back and put it on my finger. "I want to show you something else." I led him to Glad's room.

Sunlight poured through the window, which made Bright Baby's porcelain skin shine. She lay there, in the middle of the bed, just as she had before Granny Witch placed the toad on her stomach. Looking at her made the thoughts I didn't want to think reappear: Granny Witch failed. My wish was ungranted. No baby sister, no genie, only my dad. And yes, my dad was *a* wish, but not the tip-top secret one for which I'd stolen the bluebird. What I'm trying to say is, there was happiness and sadness right then, good and bad. I pulled a bead for both feelings. (I'd read about *bittersweet* in the encyclopedia.)

"Meet Bright Baby," I said.

Now, I didn't expect her to impress my dad the way the ring had. A man in a Santa suit can't know what it means to wish for a sister with every fiber of your awful, bumpy heart. Still, I wanted to show her to him. It was important he knew of her existence.

"Is that your doll?"

I shook my head. "She's Glad's."

Then we stood there, in the wash of sunlight. It would have been the perfect moment for Bright Baby to come to life, to sit up in bed and lift her porcelain hand and say with her painted strawberry mouth, *Hello there.*

But that didn't happen, so I said, "Glad died in here. In this bed."

That was another thing it was important for my dad to know.

"It took her a long time to die. At first, I was scared. I thought there'd be blood, and thrashing about, and great, pitiful wails. But there was none of that. There was just Glad, endlessly sleeping."

My dad stared at the bed and shifted from foot to foot. "She was a tough old bird," he finally said.

"Glad wasn't a bird."

"Metaphorically speaking."

There was something else I wanted to tell him.

"I'm smarter than I was the last time you came. I was only eight then. Now I'm almost eleven. Plus, I've read an entire encyclopedia set."

"Every single entry?"

"Every single entry."

"Wow." He smiled. The lines around his eyes crinkled.

I led him out of the bedroom.

He sat on the futon, and I got a kitchen stool and placed it by the coffee table so I could study him. He had dark hair, like me, and a goatee, unlike me. His nose was pointed, lips thin. He was both a stranger and the most important person in the world. I could've stared at him for hours. But people don't like to be stared at. It makes them uncomfortable. That's the truth and a point-blank fact.

My dad shifted on the futon. "When will your mom come home?"

"Soon." I decided to ask a question of my own: "Why are you wearing a Santa suit?"

"Publicity. I've begun an endeavor for which I need to attract attention."

I looked at the cats, who were lined up beside me on either side of the stool.

What are we supposed to think of this person? their eyes asked.

I wasn't sure what to tell them. He was my dad, and I loved him, but he did look rather nefarious in the tattered Santa suit.

"Are you still a DJ?" I asked. That was one of the facts I knew about him: he played music at wedding receptions.

"Of sorts," he said, which wasn't an answer. (I'd read about *evading the question* in the encyclopedia.)

I eyed the cats.

Do you want us to sic him again? they wondered.

"No," I mouthed.

And then, because I couldn't just sit on a stool and stare at my dad in silence, I said, "Were you frozen in a block of ice?" It was the only other question I could think of.

"Yes—metaphorically speaking."

"Were there penguins?"

My dad's eyes crinkled. "What do the penguins represent?"

"Birds," I said.

"Perhaps. It was dark, so I don't know for sure. I'll tell you about it when your mom gets here."

I nodded. Then I thought of all the questions a dad might ask a daughter he hadn't seen in two years. *What grade are you in? Who's your best friend? How were you able to expertly train these cats?* My dad didn't ask any questions, though. He just sat on the futon, pulling a golden disc out of his pocket.

"What's that?" I asked.

"Nothing." He put the disc away.

This was an obvious lie.

Now do you want us to sic him? the cats asked.

I had to think about it. I didn't like being lied to, but I also didn't like that I didn't like being lied to. A Tin Man wouldn't care one baby bit about a golden disc. *There's a piece of metal*, he'd think, and go on chopping with his axe.

So I told the cats no (with my eyes) and pulled a bead instead.

Then my dad and I just sat there, like two random people who only saw each other every couple of years.

Mercury sneezed. Uranus yawned. Neptune curled up on the floor and took a nap.

Then my mom walked in and screamed her head off.

Chapter 21

It's shocking, if you're a mom, to find a tattered Santa sitting on your futon. It's even more shocking when you recognize the dark goatee and crinkly eyes as belonging to your ex-husband. Screaming, you think, *That's not Santa! That's Paul!* And then you're no longer screaming out of fright but out of recognition.

"Stop!" my dad yelled. "It's me!"

Still my mom screamed.

I covered my ears. The cats ran in all directions.

"It's me!" my dad cried. "Paul!"

And then, as if my dad's name was magic, my mom stopped.

"Marta?" my dad said cautiously, like he was afraid

her name was the anti-magic that would start her screaming again.

"Paul?" my mom whispered. She was doing the breathing thing now. Deep breath in . . . deep breath out.

"I've come to see Bea-Bea," my dad said.

"It's an even year," I added, in case she'd forgotten.

My mom continued to take deep breaths. "Why are you dressed like a . . . pirate?"

"He's Santa," I said.

"I've had a conversion," said my dad.

"A conversion to what?" my mom asked.

Penguins, I thought.

"A conversion of purpose," my dad said. "Let's sit."

So we sat down at the table. The cats came out of their hiding spots and filled the empty chairs. All except Neptune, who I put on the table, even though the salad spinner wasn't out.

"The story I'm about to tell will amaze you," my dad said, "but I promise, every word is true."

I looked at the cats. They were as intrigued as I was.

"It all started down in Florida," my dad began.

"Florida?" I gasped. "You mean with Dianne?"

"Who's Dianne?"

"Her best friend," my mom said, then took a deep breath.

"No, I wasn't with Dianne. I was alone." He put his hands flat on the table, so I did, too. Our pinkies looked alike, but his thumbs were much fatter.

"It was night. I was drunk, and I was riding my bicycle down the interstate."

"Oh, Paul," my mom said sadly.

"That was pretty stupid. You could've been killed." I said this for the cats' benefit. They were easily influenced, and I didn't want them to get any bad ideas.

"It *was* stupid," said my dad. "And I *should* have been killed." He paused for dramatic effect. "But I wasn't."

"Obviously," I said.

"Don't be rude, Beatrice." My mom took another deep breath.

"I *was* hit by a car, however, and I flew from my bike and landed in a ditch. Knocked unconscious, I lay there for hours. I thought I was dead. But then my eyes opened, and I saw a million specks of light."

"Stars," I told the cats.

My dad nodded. "So I knew I was alive. I sat up. I felt my arms, legs, head. All of me was there, without injury. The only difference was this." He clenched his right hand.

"What's that mean?" I asked.

"It means I held an unknown object very tightly in my fist."

The cats began to meow excitedly, trying to guess what the object was.

My mom brought her fingers to her temples. "That's very loud, Beatrice," she said, as if I was the one doing the meowing.

"So I opened my fist," my dad said, "and saw this." He slid a hand into the pocket of his tattered red pants and pulled out the golden disc. He set it on the table.

Neptune tiptoed over and took a sniff.

"That was in your hand?" my mom asked.

"Well, not the case. But this." My dad opened the lid of the golden disc. Inside was a turquoise cushion. On the cushion was something thin and white, the size of a small paper clip.

"What is it?" I asked.

My dad's eyes crinkled. "A bone."

"*Your* bone?" my mom asked.

"*A* bone."

"Just a random bone?"

"Not random," my dad said. "It's a bone with a purpose."

"Is it *human*?" my mom asked.

"Of course," my dad said. Then he paused and whispered, "I think it belongs to a saint."

"Good grief, Paul." My mom closed her eyes, which meant she was officially *overwhelmed*.

I kept my eyes on the bone, which glowed whiter than white. I'd read about *relics* in the encyclopedia, about scraps of fabric or pieces of bone that were thought to have otherworldly powers. I'd also read about the people the relics came from: women with mysterious wounds, men who talked to wolves. There was Joan of Arc, who'd cut off her hair and put on a soldier's armor so she could lead the French army into battle. I pictured her atop a horse, clothed in metal, with not a sword but an axe.

Joan of Arc, I realized, was the original Tin Man! Maybe the bone belonged to her and had found its way to me, through my dad.

"Can I see it?" I asked, reaching for the golden disc.

My dad closed the lid and slid the case into his pocket. "Not now." He noticed the red mark on my wrist. "What's that?"

"Oh, nothing," I told him, because I didn't feel like mentioning I'd been cursed.

"She draws it on there every day with marker," my mom said. "It must be a trend."

"Ha!" I said. "I *wish* this was some stupid trend. But it's not, Dad. I've been marked. By a witch."

"Two peas in a pod," my mom whispered. "Miss Witch and Sir Saint Bone."

My dad touched the mark with his thumb. "Wash it off," he said, as if I hadn't tried hundreds of times to do just that.

"I tried," I said.

"Try harder."

Mercury raised an invisible eyebrow. *Certainly you want us to sic him now?* the eyebrow asked.

I shook my head.

"So, what are you and the saint bone up to, Paul? Still DJing?" my mom asked.

"It depends on how you define *DJing*," my dad said.

By this point, I was sick of the cryptic answers. I had stuff to do: cats to brush and wishes to get granted. "Just tell us," I said. "Were you frozen in a block of ice or not?"

"If by *frozen* you mean *stuck*, and by *block of ice* you mean *rut*, then, yes, I was most definitely frozen in a block of ice." My dad cleared his throat. "Let me begin where I left off, in the ditch with the bone in my hand. Suddenly the stars became very bright, and a voice said, *Paul, why are you playing notes on the outside when the music is within?*"

"Was that the bone talking or the alcohol?" my mom asked.

"Neither. It was—" My dad pointed at the ceiling.

And all at once I thought of Glad, not floating in the heavenly pool, but Glad as she was on Earth, at this very table, before she got sick, the Valentine's before last. She was writing a poem.

"What do you think of this?" she'd said:

"My love for you is red.
My love for you is blue.
Even when I'm miles away,
I'll still watch over you."

"Who's it for?" I asked. Even though I knew who it was for, I wanted to hear her say it.

Glad had smiled. Her hair had been the color of ashes, her face lined with the most delicate wrinkles. "You, my dear Beatrice. Always and forever you."

"So are you DJing or not?" my mom asked, interrupting the memory.

"I'm playing a different music now, the music of the bone."

"Is that so?" My mom took off her glasses and rubbed her eyes.

The cats, I could tell, were dubious. So I said, "What does bone music sound like?"

"That's the beauty of it, Bea-Bea. It sounds different for every person. It's the private tune hidden in every soul that allows them to become."

"Become what?" I asked.

"What they are meant to be." My dad reached into his pocket and pulled out the golden disc. Carefully, he opened the lid and picked up the bone with his thumb and index finger. I glanced at the boys. Even they were transfixed.

"Behold the Be Bone!" my dad cried.

"Bea like me?" I asked.

"No," he said.

"Bee like a honeybee?" I wondered.

"No. Be as in, *Be what you are meant to be, all along, from the very start.*"

"Be what you are meant to be," I whispered, and stared at the musical bone, the bone of Joan of Arc that had mysteriously appeared in my dad's fist. The boys didn't believe a word of his story; I could tell from the tilt of their heads. And I wasn't sure I believed a word of it, either. But I *wanted* to believe it.

I *needed* to believe it. What I'm trying to say is, when your best friend ignores your postcards and the witch you hired casts the wrong spell, *believing* is about the only option left.

Be what you are meant to be.

I knew what *I* was meant to be. I thought of metal. I thought of tin. I thought of how, maybe, you didn't need a witch or a genie to make your wishes come true. Maybe, if you were willing to believe, all you needed was a dad.

Neptune mewed on the tabletop. *What am I meant to be?* his plaintive eyes asked.

Exactly what you are: the furry, adorable eighth planet, my eyes shot back.

My dad put the bone away. "So that's my new mission, to get this bone to the masses. I'm on a fifty-state tour, then, who knows? Maybe I'll head down to Mexico."

"Or Antarctica," I suggested.

"How many states have you been to so far?" my mom asked.

"One."

"One?"

My dad's eyes crinkled. "This is it. The Be Bone Tour starts right here."

Chapter 22

After I begged and begged, my mom said my dad could sleep on a cot in GLAD'S while he prepared for the first tour stop. I got him a blanket and pillow. His pickup truck was parked on the street. When he pulled a suitcase out of the back, I noticed his bumper sticker. It was black, and the writing was white. Instead of letters, the words were spelled with bones.

Tired of the dead zone? Then listen to the Be Bone, the sticker said.

"Did you make that?" I asked.

"Drew it myself and had one thousand stickers printed." My dad patted the side of the suitcase. "Right in here. Five bucks apiece."

"To sell on the tour?"

"Bingo."

A shiver of excitement ran through me.

I led him into GLAD'S and helped him set up his cot. The cats gathered around and took turns sniffing his legs. He pushed them away with his shoe.

"Eight's a bit much, don't you think?" he asked.

"Are you talking about planets?"

His eyes crinkled. "No, Bea-Bea. I'm talking about cats. You've got an awful lot of cats."

"Thank you," I said, because telling a girl she has a lot of cats is the same as telling her she's pretty. That's the truth and a point-blank fact.

My dad shrugged and unzipped his suitcase. He took out the Be Bone bumper stickers and placed them on the floor in stacks. "You're going to help me, right?"

"Stack the stickers?" I asked.

My dad laughed. "No. Plan the first tour stop."

I looked at the cats, who, despite their earlier skepticism, now swished their tails with pride. My dad needed *me* to help with his mission. He had come from Florida with a beatific bone in search of a crooked-haired girl with an army of cats.

The bumps in my heart swelled so fast that I couldn't pull beads fast enough to keep up with them.

* * *

That night, I visited Bright Baby before I went to bed.

"You were supposed to come to life, but my dad showed up instead, which means Granny Witch is either a fraud or an incompetent toad handler. I'm sorry she put a dead animal on you."

The two of us were quiet. The cats had turned in for the night. My mom was watching television on the futon.

"He brought a Be Bone with him," I continued, and that same shiver of excitement rippled through me. "There's going to be an event where he'll hold it up, I think, and we'll all become what we're meant to be. The boys aren't so sure about the whole thing, but I'm going to help with the planning."

Uranus padded into the room. He looked like a ghost cat with his white fur in the nighttime shadows. He jumped onto my lap, and I stroked his back.

"Bright Baby, I've been thinking," I said. "At first, you know, I was upset my dad was here, since what I *really* wished for was you. But when he showed me the bone, I had a realization: maybe my dad's both Somebody Number Three *and* the one who'll make you come to life. I mean, nothing else I've tried has worked: not the fountain, or the birthday candle, or the star. Not even Granny Witch. But this bone my dad found, he says it's magic, and what if that's true? What if you and I could become what we're meant to be—together?"

The shiver of excitement grew so big that I had to pull a bead to stop it. I took a deep breath. "What I'm trying to say, Bright Baby, is, why not believe in the Be Bone? What have we got to lose?" I took hold of her porcelain hand. "So, what music's in your soul, sister? Something small and delicate? Maybe a minuet?" (I'd read about *classical music* in the encyclopedia.)

I scratched under Uranus's chin. "How about you? Something that sounds like a big, fat, scaly fish?"

He purred.

My own music would sound like metal. Like machines hissing, tools clanking, an axe slicing through the air.

What about you, Glad? I asked, closing my eyes. *In the heavenly pool, does music still play inside you?* I imagined her floating, a smile on her face as she listened to the humming of her soul.

I opened my eyes.

Bright Baby's eyes were open, too.

I set Uranus on the floor, then felt inside the pocket. Another note.

"*THAT*," I read. "*DO NOT TRY TO MAKE THAT—*"

Uranus meowed. He wondered if the message was complete.

"No. There's no period, see?" I held the piece of paper up for him to study. "Glad would never end a sentence without a period."

DO NOT TRY TO MAKE THAT . . .

What was Glad trying to tell me? I didn't know. But as I stood there with my ghost cat and porcelain sister, I tried harder than hard to hear the Tin Man music *clink-clank*ing in my soul.

Chapter 23

The cats wore their bow ties the next morning, in honor of my dad's arrival. They ate their breakfast quickly, hoping to get a glimpse of him before we left for school. While they lapped their water, I asked my mom what music was inside her.

She took a sip of coffee. "None."

"Not a single note?"

"No, sweetie."

"There has to be. Close your eyes and really listen."

She closed her eyes.

The cats stopped lapping, awaiting her report.

"I hear the sound of scissors not clipping and razors not buzzing and cash registers failing to ring up sales." She opened her eyes. "What I hear, Beatrice, is the sound of walls closing in—okay?"

"Not okay, Mom." I scooped up Neptune and kissed him goodbye. "Come on, boys," I told the others. Then we headed off to *The Place That Was and Always Would Be.*

First, though, I peeked in the window of GLAD'S. My dad was asleep on the cot in the middle of the beauty parlor. He'd taken off his top but still had on the red velvet pants.

It's rude to watch somebody sleep. That's the truth and a point-blank fact. There they are, a half-naked Santa with their mouth hanging open, while you're dressed, with a backpack slung over your shoulder. I watched, though, nonetheless.

"Sweet dreams, Dad," I finally said, then headed toward the traffic circle.

The cats were frisky, maybe because the sun shone and it was finally beginning to feel like spring. Instead of walking in line, they raced all around, zigzagging haphazardly. I let them. Good cat-rearing involves knowing both when to offer correction and when to just let them be.

At All That Is Amazing, we stopped for the daily checking of the window. The carnation was withered, its vase water the color of tea. The fishing line hung forlornly above it.

"I wonder why he's got a dead flower in the window," a voice said.

I turned. There was Raejean, in a shiny pink jacket.

"Awfully strange way to attract customers, don't you think?"

"I try to keep my nose out of other people's business," I said.

"*My* mom says a man in a Santa suit slept in your apartment last night."

"Your mom's wrong," I said. "He slept in the beauty parlor."

"Who is he?"

"My dad."

"Why's he dressed like Santa?"

"He came from Antarctica. That's what they wear there."

Raejean put her hands on her hips and opened her lip-glossy mouth, but before she could say anything, I said, "Horrible talking to you, Raejean-Is-Mean. Hope you're not late for school." Then I turned on my rocket blasters and shot down the sidewalk so fast that the cats had to run to keep up.

Sitting in English class, I wondered what sort of music played in Mrs. Hartley's soul. Something dull and joyless: pens marking up papers or markers sliding across whiteboards.

I decided to sharpen my pencil.

Caleb Chernavachin threw a paper football at my feet.

Back at my desk, I unfolded the note:

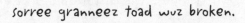

sorree granneez toad wuz broken.

r u mad at me?

This note was different from the ridiculous boy's previous notes because it asked a question. If someone asks you a question, it's rude not to answer. (I'd read about *etiquette* in the encyclopedia.) So I tore a strip of paper from my notebook and wrote:

Dear Caleb,

I'm not angry with you. How could you have known that your granny's toad was broken? I do find it regrettable, however, that she didn't have a spare. In the future, before making deals with people, she might want to be certain all her supplies are in working order.

Sincerely,
The Girl in the Back Row
(also known as Beatrice)

I folded the paper in the shape of a cat head while Mrs. Hartley explained the difference between adjectives and adverbs. Then I sharpened my pencil again and dropped the note on Caleb's desk.

Back at my own desk, I began writing an essay Mrs. Hartley assigned on "A Very Important Moment in My Life." A few minutes later, I glanced up and saw a triangular object whiz through the air. It landed on my desk.

Caleb raised his arms victoriously.

"Mr. Chernavachin, are you having a muscular spasm?" Mrs. Hartley asked.

The class tittered as Caleb hung his head. I unfolded the note.

yr dad seemed rilly kool. can i see him agin?

Another question. I tore a second strip of paper.

Dear Caleb,

Yes, I'd be willing to formally introduce you to my dad. Meet me outside when the bell rings and be prepared to answer this question: what is the music in your soul? My dad is on a mission and doesn't have time to talk to people who haven't thought deeply on this subject.

Sincerely,
TGITBR (aka Beatrice)

I folded the paper into a cat head, then worked on my essay for a few minutes. I'd decided to write it from the future.

A very important moment in my life was when I attended the first stop of the Be Bone Tour. Up until that moment, I'd been an average girl with a sad, annoying, extra-bumpy heart. But when my dad held up the Be Bone and said the magic words, there was a gust of wind and a flash of light, and my body turned to **METAL.**

I wrote *metal* in capital letters, traced it twice, and underlined it three times, which caused my pencil lead to snap.

"Guess I'll have to go to the sharpener again," I whispered to the girl beside me.

She put a finger to her lips. "Shh."

I picked up the cat head and dropped it on Caleb's desk.

"This is your third trip to the sharpener, Beatrice," said Mrs. Hartley. "Do you have an unusually weak pencil, or are you thinking of excuses to drop notes on Mr. Chernavachin's desk?"

The question was rhetorical, so I gave no answer while the class laughed. Raejean threw her head back so far that it looked like it might snap off her neck.

Unfortunately, it didn't.

Which meant, when I walked by her, she was able to whisper, "K-I-S-S-I-N-G."

Tin Men don't know how to spell, though, so I ignored her.

Chapter 24

"Leprechauns," Caleb said when I met him after the final bell.

"What?" I said. It was warm and the cats were sunbathing in the grass.

"That's what I hear in my soul. Leprechauns."

"Leprechauns aren't music."

"Yeah, but they can *make* music."

"How?"

"With bongo drums."

I scoffed. "Leprechauns don't play bongo drums. They play harps."

"Aw, come on!" Caleb said. "That's not true."

I decided to change the subject. "Why are you still wearing that coat? It's March. Aren't you hot?"

Caleb pulled his earlobe. "My dad gave it to me."

"So?"

"It's the only thing he ever gave me." He looked off in the distance, like there might be something interesting very far away.

I tried to think if my dad had ever given me anything. He hadn't. But that was about to change—thanks to the Be Bone. So I pulled a bead for myself, in expectation of the gift I was about to receive, and I pulled one for Caleb, who suspected he'd never get another. Then I said, "Come on, boys," and the nine of us headed home.

On the way, Caleb said, "Do we need to go by the fountain?"

I shook my head. "I'm done with fountains. I've got *real* magic now."

"What's that mean?"

"You'll find out."

We did stop in front of All That Is Amazing.

"That's one dead petunia," Caleb said, looking at the shriveled flower in the window.

"It's a carnation, and I think it's pretty."

Caleb stared at me. "You're jokin', right?"

I let my silence indicate that I wasn't.

Felix saw us from behind the counter. He waved, and Caleb waved back, so I grabbed his arm.

"Don't perform perfunctory rituals for *Men Who Make FOR SALE Signs*," I said.

"What's that mean?"

"It means don't be nice to him."

Caleb shrugged. "Whatever."

So we stood, unwaving, and stared at Felix while the witch mark burned like fire on my wrist.

Nancy, the insurance agent, was getting a pity cut inside GLAD'S. A purple cape was fastened around her neck, and her eyes were closed so she couldn't see what my mom was doing to her. Sprinkles, the poodle, sat beside her, a matching cape around his own furry neck.

"I'm home," I said. I stood with my back to the FOR SALE sign.

My mom had a plastic comb between her teeth. In her hands were a bowl of mayonnaise and a paintbrush. She nodded in my direction and mumbled something that sounded like, "My meatie."

Nancy opened one eye and peeked at me. "Hello, Beatrice."

I decided to ask her the question. "What kind of music do you hear in your soul?"

My mom spit the comb onto the floor. "Beatrice, this isn't philosophy class—okay? People come here to relax, not to be peppered with questions."

"I'm not peppering."

"Oh, I don't mind." Nancy waved her hand beneath her purple cape. "Let me think." She closed her eyes again. "I hear the sound of insurance policies being purchased to protect one's most valuable assets from fire, theft, or flood."

Caleb pulled his earlobe. "What's that sound like?"

"Security."

"How lovely," my mom said.

Caleb and I left then. I flashed the witch mark at the FOR SALE sign on the way out the door, and the cats arched their backs in contempt.

Up in the apartment, I checked the mail on the kitchen table as Neptune ran to greet me. My dad was waiting on the futon, dressed like a normal human, in jeans and a T-shirt.

This is the truth and a point-blank fact: it's shocking to step into a place and see a person who's usually missing where he's supposed to be. To have my dad there, waiting for me, was like witnessing a miracle. The shiver of excitement surged through me, and I had to pull a bead to calm down.

"Bea-Bea!" my dad said.

"Dad, this is Caleb Chernavachin."

"How do you do?" Caleb bowed as if he were meeting a king.

"Did you come to help with the Be Bone Tour?" my dad asked.

"I haven't told him about it yet," I said.

"How's he going to help with something if he doesn't know it exists?" My dad reached into his pocket and pulled out the golden disc. He opened the lid.

Caleb, the cats, and I stepped closer to marvel at its glow.

"This is the bone of a saint," my dad said. "It was given to me in a moment of darkness, along with a task: share it and its message with the world."

"Can I touch it?" Caleb asked.

"Not now, but at the appropriate time, all who are inclined may come forward to *become*."

"That's why it's the Be Bone," I explained. "It helps you *be* what you're meant to be, way down deep inside."

"I'm meant to be a wrestler," Caleb said. Then he added, "I'm real rich, you know."

"Great," my dad said. "You can buy a sticker." He winked at me. "Now, I'll tell you what I'm thinking.

I'm thinking a stage and a tent, right there, in the traffic circle. I'm thinking a banner that says *Become What You Are.*"

"With letters made of bones?" I asked.

"Bingo," said my dad.

"Oh, man!" Caleb pumped his fist. "That'll be cool!"

"But what we need," my dad said, "is some sort of activity to draw people in, something we can advertise to get people interested."

"How about a wrestlin' match?" Caleb suggested.

"No," I said. "Only ridiculous boys want to watch a wrestling match. What about a cat show?"

Caleb scowled. "No. Only crooked-haired cat-girls wanna see a cat show."

"I got it!" my dad said. "An Easter egg hunt."

"With prizes?" I asked.

"With prizes."

"Oh, man!" Caleb said.

"Plus, one grand prize," said my dad, "worth a thousand dollars."

Caleb bounced on his heels. "Oh, man! Oh, man!"

"What's the grand prize?" I asked.

My dad's eyes crinkled. "Not sure, Bea-Bea. I'll figure that part out later. Today we're making posters."

I got the art supplies and a stack of paper, and the

three of us sat down. The cats leapt onto the tabletop and carefully tiptoed across its surface.

"You've sure got a lot of cats, Bea-Bea."

"We established that fact yesterday, Dad."

"They stink," Caleb said, plugging his nose.

"No, they don't!" I kicked him under the table.

"Ow!"

"You watch your mouth," I seethed, "or they'll tear that puffy coat of yours to pieces."

"Children," my dad said, "stop fighting. We have a hundred posters to make."

"A hundred!" Caleb cried.

"Can't we make copies?" I asked.

"There's no budget for copies," my dad said. "We'll have to make them by hand."

Mercury, who sat across from me, squinted his golden eyes. *How can a man who can't afford copies come up with a thousand-dollar prize?* he wondered.

I squinted my own eyes in return. *He'll figure that out later,* I said.

My dad wrote down the poster details for us to copy, but I suggested that Caleb, who thought *granny* ended in two *e*'s, leave the spelling to me. He could be the illustrator.

Tired of living in the dead zone? Come listen to the Be Bone, I wrote in big red letters.

Mystical bone's first stop on 50-state tour!
Easter egg hunt! Grand prize: $1,000
Saturday, 2 p.m., in the traffic circle

I read what I'd written over and over again, and every single time, my heart swelled so big, I thought it might explode. What were the chances, out of all the men in the world, my dad would be *my* dad? And what were the chances, out of all the bones in the world, that the exact bone I needed would end up *right here*?

It was fate. It was magic. It was the granting, finally, of a wish.

"Wait!" my dad said.

I paused, red marker hovering in the air.

"I'm going to need an opening act, to warm up the crowd before I reveal the bone."

Neptune meowed from his spot on my lap.

I looked down at him. *Really?* my eyes asked. I turned to the other cats. "Are you guys sure?" I meant to say it with my eyes but accidentally said it with my mouth.

"Are we sure about what?" Caleb asked.

I looked at my dad. "I've taught the cats a dance routine. They could be the opening act."

Caleb smirked. "Yeah, right."

My dad raised a skeptical eyebrow. "Show me."

I called the cats from the table and arranged them into formation. Crouching beside them, I whispered, "Don't let me down." Then I stood up.

"The fish swims this way." I wiggled my hand to the right. The cats took a step. "The fish swims that way." They stepped to the left. "The fish swims far." The cats stepped back. "The fish swims near." They stepped forward. "A worm is on the hook!" They swished their tails and meowed.

"Oh, man!" Caleb said. "That was like a TV commercial."

"Excellent work, Bea-Bea," said my dad. "That's the opening act, right there. Now, what shall we call them?"

"I know!" Caleb cried. "The Leprechaun's Pets."

"If you mention leprechauns one more time, Caleb Chernavachin . . . ," I said.

"How about Corwell's Killer Cats?" my dad asked.

"They're not killers."

"They kind of look like killers."

I stared at the cats, who were still arranged in perfect formation. They didn't look like killers. They looked the opposite of killers, like the nicest, most peaceful creatures in the world.

Venus winked at me. The wink meant: *You can call us killers. We don't mind.*

But *I* minded. I pictured the boys in my bedroom, gently sleeping atop my solar system bedspread. I didn't want the whole town to think they were *criminals*. "Wait! I've got it. How about Corwell's *Cosmic Cats*?"

My dad's eyes crinkled. "I love it."

So I picked up my red marker. *Featuring Corwell's Cosmic Cats!* I wrote at the bottom of the poster. Then I had to pull four beads because I'd never felt so happy in my life.

Chapter 25

We made posters till my mom came home. *We're GLAD You're Here*, said her shirt, but her mouth did not. Her mouth said, "I can barely afford to feed Beatrice. There's no way I can feed you, too, Paul."

"I wouldn't dare suggest it," my dad said, rising from the table. "I'll get my cot and head downstairs."

"I gotta go, too," said Caleb. "My mom got promoted at work, and we're havin' a big celebration."

So then it was just me, my mom, and the cats.

"How was your day, sweetie?" she asked as she put noodles in a pot.

"Life-changing." I showed her one of the posters and told her the cats would be the opening act, and there'd be an egg hunt with a thousand-dollar prize.

She stopped stirring the noodles. "Where's Paul Corwell, the man who showed up in a tattered Santa suit, going to get a thousand-dollar prize?"

"The Santa suit wasn't tattered when he showed up," I corrected her. "It was a perfectly respectable outfit until the boys attacked him."

My mom closed her eyes and started the breathing thing. There was a glob of mayonnaise on her glasses. "What I'm asking is, what will happen when people show up for an egg hunt, and there's no grand prize?"

"There will be a grand prize."

"No, there won't, and then your dad will go to jail."

"Jail?" I gasped.

"It's called fraud, sweetie—okay? You can't advertise you're giving away a thousand-dollar prize if you don't have a thousand-dollar prize to give."

I stared at her while a picture of my dad dressed in a Santa suit and sitting in a jail cell flashed in my mind.

My mom touched my elbow. "I'm not trying to scare you. I just—I don't know what your dad's up to. And *whatever* he's up to, I don't want you to get hurt. See what I mean?"

I didn't. All I saw was my dad behind a wall of bars

with a metal chain around his ankle. I pulled a bead and shook the picture from my head. Then I changed the subject. "Did anyone call about stealing Glad's beauty parlor?"

"*Buying* it, you mean? No."

"Good," I said, and walked away as my mom took one of her deep breaths.

I'd realized something. My mom was too stressed out to believe in the Be Bone, which meant she wouldn't hear the music deep within. Which meant she wouldn't become what she was meant to be. She'd forever stay what she now was: *overwhelmed*, with mayonnaise on her glasses.

It's not a good feeling to have a realization like that, so it was with solemn faces that the cats and I went to Glad's room. I slid out the chair and began to pull bead after bead, lightning fast.

After a while, I said to Bright Baby, "I haven't forgotten you. The posters are taking up a lot of my time. I didn't even have a chance to write Dianne of the Flame-Red Hair today because I was so busy passing notes with Caleb."

Next, I sent a message to the heavenly pool. *I haven't forgotten you, either, Glad. I'll carry you around forever, even when I'm made of tin. And I'll*

never let Mom sell your beauty parlor, so don't worry about that.

Bright Baby's eyes popped open. Jupiter tiptoed across the bed and batted at her pocket.

I pulled out the note. It said: *WHICH.*

"DO NOT TRY TO MAKE THAT WHICH—"

At the word *which*, the cats hissed and arched their backs.

I laughed. "Not *WITCH* like, *Granny Witch is a good-for-nothing, toad-killing imposter.* But *WHICH* like, *WHICH would you rather be: a sad girl or a fearless Tin Man?*"

The cats looked confused, but that was okay because I was confused by Glad's message, too. What if language was different in heaven? What if Glad thought she was telling me something important, but the message here on Earth didn't make any sense?

"DO NOT TRY TO MAKE THAT WHICH—"

Poor little Neptune hissed again.

I picked him up and pressed him to my mouth. "I love you."

I looked at Bright Baby's pretty blue eyes. "I love you, too."

And then I thought of Glad, hair splayed on the water, floating. *I love you three. And three, just so you know, means forever.*

Raejean was waiting at the bottom of the stairs the next morning. She had her backpack on one shoulder, and on her free arm hung Montgomery in the pink leather purse.

"You can't take your dog to school," I said.

"Why not? You take your nine cats." Her hair was parted straight down the middle, with an awful curl hanging in each eye.

"Learn to count, Raejean. I have *eight* cats. And I don't take them to school. Seven of them *escort* me, without entering the building."

"Well, Montgomery and I are having a morning perambulation," Raejean said. "I bet you don't even know what that means."

"Oh, please. I've read a twenty-six-volume encyclopedia set. *Perambulation* is for babies."

I looked at Montgomery, in the purse with his tongue sticking out. I felt sorry for him, that he had to ride around on the arm of someone as horrible as Raejean.

"*My* mom says your dad got a permit to hold an event in the traffic circle."

I shrugged. *Perhaps that's true,* my shoulders said, *but perhaps it's not.*

"*My* mom says that bone your dad has is nothing but a chicken bone. *My* mom says your dad is a charlatan."

My temper flared like a fire. "My dad is not a fraud! You take it back, Raejean-Is-Mean!"

Raejean smiled her awful, fake smile. "Never, Beatrice-Feet-Kiss."

So I pushed her.

She landed on her backside, on the sidewalk. Montgomery let out a surprised yip.

"You'll be sorry," I said, "when we're all hunting eggs, and you're stuck at home, brushing your dog's fur!"

"You and your cats couldn't find an egg if it was hidden on the end of your nose!" Raejean screamed.

"Joke's on you! My cats are the opening act!"

"The opening act for a charlatan with a chicken bone!"

"Name a single song that plays in your soul," I demanded.

Raejean stared at me, mouth open, curls in her eyes.

I turned to the cats. "That's what I thought. She's *musicless.*"

Then I switched on my rocket blasters and shot out of there, pulling bead after bead as I zoomed down the sidewalk, faster than fast.

At *The Place That Was and Always Would Be*, Caleb
wrote me a note:

can I help u and ur dad make mor postirs?

Since it was a question, I was forced to compose
yet another reply, which I did stealthily while Mrs.
Hartley made a list of intransitive verbs.

Dear Caleb,
You may help us again, on two conditions:
You may not say my cats stink (because
it isn't true). And you may not mention
leprechauns. Your obsession with the
fantastical creatures is exhausting.
        Sincerely,
        The Touring Manager of
        Corwell's Cosmic Cats
        (commonly known as Beatrice)

I folded the note into a cat head, then grabbed my pencil and walked over to the sharpener.

"Name an intransitive verb, Beatrice," Mrs. Hartley said, because she thought I wasn't paying attention.

"Sleep." (Little did she know, I'd read about *multi-tasking* in the encyclopedia.)

Raejean laughed scornfully, but Caleb flashed a thumbs-up as I dropped the cat head on his desk.

I took a seat and spent the rest of the day doodling in my notebook: pictures of Tin Men and baby sisters and bones that glowed brighter than bright.

Chapter 26

*A*new routine started. Every day, Caleb and I walked home from school together to help my dad make posters. We worked till my mom came home, at which point my dad and Caleb left, and my mom said something like, "How many of those are you going to make?"

"One hundred," I'd tell her.

"That seems excessive."

"You can never have too much publicity, is what Dad says."

"Does he?" she'd say, and take a deep, *overwhelmed* breath, then start dinner. But soon she'd turn around and say, "I don't like the way he's using you."

"He's not using me. I'm voluntarily assisting him with full understanding of the situation."

"I just don't want you to get hurt—okay?"

"I won't. Besides, pretty soon I'll be indestructible."

My mom pressed her lips together and looked sad.

Without thinking, I said, "Tin Men don't cry. They'll rust."

Her expression changed from sad to confused. "What do *Tin Men* have to do with anything?"

I pretended I didn't hear her.

"He's not staying, sweetie," she said. "I hate to be the bearer of bad news, but he'll leave as soon as whatever this thing he's doing is over."

"It's called a tour stop, Mom. And I know."

My mom didn't listen. She just kept talking, like there was a whole bunch of words she had to say, and she wasn't going to let anyone stop her.

"Paul's doing what he always does: swoops in every couple of years, gets people all riled up, then disappears to who knows where."

"Do I look riled up, Mom?"

My mom didn't turn around to see. "That man will end up in jail," she said, then kept on peeling potatoes, shoulders rising and falling with each *overwhelmed* breath.

* * *

It took several more days, but then finally it really, truly felt like spring. Since Tin Men don't have skin, they can't perceive fluctuations in temperature, but I couldn't help noticing that Caleb was pink-faced and sweating in his puffy coat.

"I think your dad wouldn't mind if you stopped wearing it, now that winter's over," I told him.

We were on the sidewalk in front of All That Is Amazing, on our way home from *The Place That Was and Always Would Be*. The cats were crowded around our feet.

"I gotta keep it on 'cause I want him to see I still got it when he comes back," Caleb said, sweat trickling down his forehead.

"Can't you just show it to him, hanging in your closet?"

"A coat hangin' in a closet is different from a coat bein' worn."

And while that was true, I couldn't see why it meant he had to sweat to death. But I kept my mouth shut and looked in Felix's store window, at what was left of the carnation.

"It's just a stick," Caleb said.

He was right. All the petals had fallen off. Only a brown stalk remained.

"Poor petunia." Caleb tugged his earlobe.

"Poor petunia," I echoed, because Tin Men know nothing about flowers.

Before we climbed the apartment stairs, I said, "He's not going to stay, just so you know."

"Who's not gonna stay?" Caleb asked.

"My dad. When the Be Bone Tour is over, he'll leave."

"How do you know?"

"He always leaves."

"But *always* doesn't mean every single time."

"Yes, it does, Caleb. That's exactly what *always* means."

Caleb frowned. He looked like he might cry. "Where's he gonna go?"

"Back to Antarctica. To feed the penguins."

"I thought he *ate* them."

"He feeds them first."

Caleb looked down at his sneakers and wiggled the toes sticking out of the holes. "But I wanna keep makin' posters," he said glumly.

"We can't make posters forever."

"Yeah, we can. Like, for holidays and stuff."

I shook my head and happened to catch Venus's grim stare. *What a pitiable boy*, his yellow eyes said.

Caleb ran a hand through his porcupine quills and puffed out his puffy-coated chest. "Well, this time's gonna be different. He's stayin'."

"Not different. Not staying." I pulled a bead on his behalf.

Sometimes I forgot to write to Dianne of the Flame-Red Hair, and sometimes I was just too busy. I had only a couple of postcards left, which meant I'd looked at that cardinal's steely eyes so many times, I found them bland. Plus, I was running out of ideas.

Dear D.,
OHIO = TRILOBITE
FLORIDA = SAND
Take your pick.
                    Love,
                    B.

Rereading the message, I knew it wasn't my best, but the thing was, I didn't really care.

"Did you secure the thousand-dollar prize?" I asked my dad one day.

I'd just finished writing *Featuring Corwell's Cosmic Cats!* in an elegant script. Beside me, Caleb was illustrating another poster by drawing eight smiling cat faces.

"It's been secured from the start," my dad said.

"What is it?" Caleb asked, eyes flashing.

"I don't know."

I looked at Caleb. *Huh?* his face said.

I looked at the cats. *How can he have secured the prize if he doesn't know what it is?* their expressions asked.

"If a bone can appear in my hand, there's no reason a prize can't appear in an egg," my dad said.

"But the bone's different," I told him. "The bone is a one-in-a-million event. Prizes don't just appear in eggs, Dad. Somebody's got to put them there."

"We'll see," he said.

At that moment two things happened: Neptune raced across the table, slid on a row of markers, and rolled, as if on a skateboard, to the floor. Plus, I realized my mom was right. There was no prize. Which meant my dad was going to jail.

Chapter 27

On the day we finished the hundredth poster, Caleb burst into tears.

"What's wrong with him?" my dad asked, arranging the papers in a neat stack.

Caleb folded his puffy arms on the table, lowered his face, and wept.

"He doesn't want to stop helping you," I said.

"Good! *Making* the posters was only step one. Now it's time for step two."

Caleb raised his head. His freckles were covered in tears. "What's step two?" he sniffed.

"Hanging them," my dad said.

"Oh, man!" Caleb cried. "Oh, man!"

The cats purred because they were the types who delighted in others' happiness.

We went out with rolls of masking tape on our wrists and stacks of posters in our hands. The boys were bow-tied and pranced in line behind us. (Even Neptune was old enough to come along now.) The plan was that Caleb and I would hang posters downtown while my dad used his truck to place posters in the stores that weren't within walking distance.

I hung one on the GLAD'S window first, right on top of the FOR SALE sign. Then we went from shop to shop, asking if we could put a poster in the window.

At All That Is Amazing, I said, "Let's skip this one."

"You scared?" Caleb asked, peering at me from beneath his porcupine quills.

"Why would I be scared of Felix Farmer?"

"'Cause he knows what you did."

"He doesn't."

"He might," Caleb said.

"You did it, too."

"No, I didn't. I just wrestled him in back."

That made me mad. "You were an accomplice, Caleb Chernavachin, which is in itself a crime." (I'd read about the *penal code* in the encyclopedia.)

"Nobody told me that."

"Ignorance of the law is no excuse, you puffy nin-compoop." I pushed him in the chest.

"Keep your hands to yourself, you crooked-haired cat-girl." Caleb jabbed me with his elbow.

That made me madder still, so I said, "I'm going in there because I'm not scared of Felix Farmer *one bit*."

"Meow," Saturn cried in warning.

But I'd already said it, so I had to do it, or Caleb would think I was a chicken. So I pulled open the door, and all ten of us went in.

Felix looked up from the counter.

"Mercury, Venus, Earth, Mars, Jupiter, Saturn, Uranus, Neptune, Caleb, and Beatrice," he said. "How nice to see you."

But it isn't nice to see someone who betrayed you and whom you betrayed in return. It's the opposite of nice. It's horrible. That's the truth and a point-blank fact.

"Can we hang a poster in your window?" I asked.

"You mean where the bluebird flew?"

I looked at Caleb.

"Run," he mouthed.

But a Tin Man wouldn't run. A Tin Man would stand there, all cold, hard metal, and say, "Yes."

"Let me see it," Felix said.

Caleb handed him a poster.

The cats jumped up on the counter, and Felix petted them while he read. "What's a Be Bone?" he asked.

"Her dad found it. It's magic-like," Caleb said.

Felix looked at me. "So he did come back before you turned eleven."

I nodded.

"I'm happy to hear it." He returned his attention to the poster. "And these, I suppose, are the cosmic cats?"

"Yes," I said.

"And they're going to perform some type of act?"

"They can dance!" Caleb cried. "Oh, man! You should see 'em."

Felix stared at me, and I stared at him. His silver earrings glinted, but his eyes said nothing, so mine said nothing back.

"There's gonna be an egg hunt, too, with a big prize," Caleb said.

"So I read." Felix handed the poster to Caleb. "Sure. You can put it up. Just don't block the carnation."

I climbed into the window display and taped up the poster. I hung it so that, looking in from the outside, you couldn't see where the bluebird had been.

On the sidewalk, Caleb said, "That looks weird."

And it did look weird to see a fishing line that

ended in a poster with a dead brown stalk beneath it. It looked very weird and also very sad.

We hung posters all afternoon, telling people about the Be Bone and Corwell's Cosmic Cats. Caleb liked to mention the thousand-dollar prize, though I didn't, because it made me think of my dad, locked in a jail cell and wearing a shredded Santa suit.

We saved Cutie Pie Camera for last. Instead of going inside, we stood on the sidewalk and stared in the window.

There was a whole big family in there: a mom, a dad, two boys, a girl, and a grandma and grandpa. They all had on white T-shirts and blue jeans and sat on fake grass. Raejean's mom gave each of them a plastic poppy.

"What a stupid picture," Caleb said.

"Yeah," I agreed. "I'm sure happy I'm not in that family."

The family smiled big, fake plastic-poppy smiles. They looked like the kind of people who'd never woken up in a ditch with a bone in their hand. They didn't have crooked haircuts and had probably never taught their cats to dance.

Raejean was nowhere to be seen, but Montgomery was inside the photography studio, running in circles, trying to bite his own tail. When he saw me, he raced to the door and stood at the glass with his tongue hanging out.

The cats stepped forward to investigate, and I did, too, crouching on the sidewalk.

"That's not a real dog. That's a robot," Caleb said.

"No, he's real. Aren't you, Montgomery?" I pressed my thumb against the glass, and the Pomeranian tried to lick it.

"Well, ain't he cute?" a dry, dug-up-from-the-dirt voice said.

There, in the glass, stood Granny Witch's shadowy reflection.

Chapter 28

Granny Witch looked bigger than before, in her grizzly-bear fur coat and tube top. Her hair was puffier. Red feathers dangled from her ears.

"Look at that." She crouched beside me and tapped a long green fingernail on the glass.

Montgomery let out a yip and jumped back.

Granny Witch laughed. "Ha ha ha! He'd fit in here, I bet." Under her arm was the toad case.

Now, Raejean was no one's friend. But the thought of Montgomery riding around with a dead toad on the arm of a witch was more than even the tinniest of Tin Men could stand.

"You can't have him," I said.

Granny Witch turned her witchy eyes on me. She

was so close I could smell the damp, earthworm scent of her flesh.

"Says who?" she asked.

"Beatrice Corwell."

Quick as a snake, she grabbed my arm. "You mean the girl with the mark on her wrist?" She rubbed her thumb over the red stain:

"I get what I want
And I want what I see
And the girl I marked
Will never stop me."

She flung my wrist away, then stood up and pointed her nose toward the sky. "Smells like tornado. Come on, Caleb."

"Aw, man," Caleb whined, but he had no choice but to follow his big, bad granny home.

"We hung the posters," I told my mom at dinner.

"Did you find a thousand-dollar prize?" she asked.

"No. Did you sell Glad's beauty parlor?"

"No."

We chewed our food.

"Do you think you'd recognize me if I was made of tin?"

My mom's fork froze halfway to her mouth. "What?"

"If I was all shiny silver and covered in metal, do you think you'd know who I was?"

"If you still asked such bizarre questions, then, yes."

"Good. I'd hate for you to run from me in horror."

"Oh, sweetie, I would never run from you in horror," my mom said, patting my hand. "No matter what type of metal you were covered in."

That night I sat with the cats and talked to Bright Baby.

"I think Granny Witch put another curse on me," I told her, "but I'm not worried. Her spells are about as worthless as Raejean's smiles."

I watched Bright Baby sleep for a while. Then I said, "Pretty soon, you and I are going to get exactly what we want. And just so you know: when my heart turns to metal, I'll still love you. I'm going to leave one bump that's just for you."

I closed my eyes and sent a message to Glad. *I'll still love you, too, Glad. Don't you worry.* I was quiet then, imagining Glad in the heavenly pool. When I opened my eyes, Bright Baby's were also open. I removed the note from her pocket.

BEATS, it said.

"DO NOT TRY TO MAKE THAT WHICH BEATS—"

The cats looked as disappointed as I felt.

"Oh, Glad," I cried. "Are you paying attention? Do you think I'm trying to make a drum?"

I'd read about *disappointment* in the encyclopedia, but to read about a thing is different from experiencing it. Experiencing is what pulling beads was made for.

Mrs. Hartley made us read our "A Very Important Moment in My Life" essays in front of the class. Raejean went first.

"A very important moment in my life was when I got my Pomeranian puppy for Christmas. Purebred dogs are very expensive. Not a lot of people can afford them. Some have to settle for stray cats." She paused to look at me, then went back to reading. "But my family has a lot of money because Cutie Pie Camera is so successful. That's why we can buy purebred puppies."

Raejean did a fake curtsy, and everyone clapped.

Caleb got up next.

"A very important moment in my life was when my mom told me my dad was famous. Up until that moment, I thought he was just a normal person. But then she showed me magazines with his face on the cover, and then she showed me a vault filled with money. The last thing she showed me was our swimming pool, which was filled with hundred-dollar bills instead of water. We put on our swimsuits and swam around in it, and then we ate some, too, because we had so much money we could do whatever we wanted."

"Why would you eat your money?" Raejean asked.

"Eating money is beside the point," Mrs. Hartley said. "Don't forget, class: these are supposed to be *true* stories."

"It *is* true." Caleb scowled.

Everybody laughed except me. I said, "I believe you, Caleb Chernavachin," but he couldn't hear me over the hyenas.

Then a kid got up who said a very important moment in his life was when he poured a bowl of Lucky Charms and all the marshmallows were shaped like pickles. A girl said her very important moment was when her mom let her wear safety pins in her pierced ears.

Finally, it was my turn.

"My very important moment takes place in the future," I said.

"Are you a fortune teller?" Mrs. Hartley asked.

The class laughed.

I didn't care. I told them how, in the future, I would attend the Be Bone's first tour stop. I told how my dad would raise the bone above my head, and there'd be a gust of wind and a flash of light, and then my skin would turn to metal.

"Like a robot?" asked the boy who got the marshmallow pickles.

"No, not a *robot*. A Tin Man."

They all stared at me. They didn't laugh. They didn't clap. They just stared, like I was some girl with crooked hair who they didn't know what on earth she was talking about.

"You may take a seat, Beatrice," Mrs. Hartley said.

So I sat down and quietly reread my essay. Then I drew two lines at the top of the page: I I . That's how many days were left until Bright Baby and I would become what we were meant to be.

I could hardly stand it.

Caleb waited with the cats outside *The Place That Was and Always Would Be*.

"That'll be real cool when you're all covered in metal," he said.

I nodded and picked up Neptune. "I bet that was fun, swimming in those hundred-dollar bills."

Caleb grinned.

"What did they taste like?"

"Aw, nothin', really. Lettuce, I guess."

"Caleb, I have to tell you something that you're not going to want to hear."

"What?"

"My dad's taking me to buy eggs for the egg hunt tonight, and I want to go by myself, just me and him."

"Oh." He looked down at his holey sneakers.

"I haven't gotten to spend a lot of time with him on my own, you know?"

Caleb was quiet and kept his head hung down.

"And he'll be leaving in a few days—"

Caleb looked up. "You don't know that."

"I do," I said. "I really do."

Caleb crossed his puffy arms and scowled.

"You can help me fill the eggs with candy."

"Nah," he said. "I can't."

"Why not?"

He shrugged, then looked up at the sky. "You wanna know a very important moment in my life?"

He didn't wait for an answer. "It's when I first saw you, in your pj's, tryin' to rescue that stinky cat."

"Neptune doesn't stink."

Caleb pulled his earlobe. "See you later, Beatrice Corwell."

"After a while, Caleb Chernavachin."

We looked at each other for a long time, not talking, just staring, like this was some kind of final goodbye. Like we'd never see each other again.

Chapter 29

I tried not to be excited, riding in the truck with my dad. I tried to think like a Tin Man: *I am made of metal. This truck is made of metal. Metal inside of metal. Ho hum.* But I couldn't make it ho-hum no matter how hard I tried—because sitting in a truck with my dad was like being on a Ferris wheel: a fantastic occurrence that didn't happen very often, so you better enjoy the ride.

I pulled a bead, rolled down my window, and felt the wind lift my hair. "This truck is fast, Dad, and I like it."

My dad's eyes crinkled. "This truck is old, Bea-Bea, but I like it, too."

"How many eggs are we going to buy?"

"Five hundred."

"Marvelous!" That's exactly what five hundred plastic eggs would be: a marvelous sight to behold. I didn't mention the thousand-dollar prize because, when you're riding on a Ferris wheel, it's best to keep unpleasant things unsaid. I touched my dad's elbow. "I'm happy you came."

"I always do."

The shiver ran through me then, filling my bones with excitement. "What do you think will happen when you hold up the Be Bone and somebody hears the music in their soul for the first time?"

"I think it'll be a game changer," my dad said.

I looked out my window. *A game changer.* I wished the game had changed already, and Bright Baby was in the truck, our hair flying out the window together.

I turned back to my dad. "When are you leaving?"

"Sunday."

The day after the tour. That's what I'd told Caleb. But telling somebody something is different from it being told to you.

"I'll miss you. I always miss you, Dad. Even right now, even though you're beside me, I miss you. It's like missing you is all I know how to do."

"I'm still here, Bea-Bea. No need to miss me yet."

I nodded because that was true. And what was also

true was that the time had almost come. My bumpy old heart had less than forty-eight hours left.

The next day, Caleb didn't show up at *The Place That Was and Always Would Be*. It was the first day he was absent. I stared at his empty desk for so long that Mrs. Hartley said, "Beatrice, is it safe to assume you find Mr. Chernavachin's chair more interesting than your spelling list?"

Everybody laughed except Raejean, because Raejean also wasn't there.

At recess, a boy with a rabid-looking rat on his shirt came up to me and said, "Did you hear what happened to Raejean's store?"

"Raejean doesn't have a store," I said. "Her *parents* have a store."

"Don't be weird, Beatrice," Rabid Rat Boy said.

"I'm not being weird. I'm being factual."

Rabid Rat Boy looked at me like he didn't know what *factual* meant. So, because I was curious, I asked, "What happened to Raejean's store?" even though the question was not factually accurate.

"It was robbed!" he cried. "Somebody smashed the glass and wiped out the cash register."

"Oh no."

"Oh yes! There was crime scene tape on the door and police cars in the street, and Raejean's mom was crying. I saw it on the news!"

"Do they know who did it?" I asked.

"No! The robber remains *at large*!" Rabid Rat Boy yelled, then scurried away to spread the news throughout the playground.

When we came back from recess, Mrs. Hartley wrote *How does the robbery of Cutie Pie Camera make you feel?* on the board. We were supposed to call out adjectives for her to write down.

"There are no wrong answers," she said.

"Scared."

"Excited."

"Nervous."

She pointed at me.

"Metallic."

Mrs. Hartley frowned, but she wrote *metallic*, very small, with a question mark.

I nodded mechanically, in a Tin Man fashion, but the truth and point-blank fact was this: I didn't feel metallic. I felt like I wished Caleb Chernavachin hadn't picked this day out of all days to be absent.

Staring at his empty chair made me realize something. I missed Caleb. I missed him more than I missed Dianne of the Flame-Red Hair.

Somehow, the most ridiculous boy in the world had become my best friend.

"A crime has been committed," I told the cats after the final bell rang.

Their expressions were a mixture of the adjectives on Mrs. Hartley's board: scared, excited, nervous. (Not metallic, because there's no such thing as Tin Cats.)

I turned on my rocket blasters, and the nine of us raced to Cutie Pie Camera, faster than fast. The police cars were gone. So was the police tape. There was a piece of plywood where the door's glass had been.

There were no families inside. The lights were off. But Raejean was in there. When she saw me on the sidewalk, she came outside. Her face was covered in pink splotches, and her eyes were teary.

"The robber took Montgomery. I bet you're happy," she said, and sniffed.

The cats and I were aghast. "Why would I be happy about that?"

"Because you've never liked me or my dog!" Rae-jean cried.

Now, it was true I didn't like Raejean, but I had nothing against Montgomery. It would be rude, under the circumstances, to tell her the first part, though, so I just said, "I'm sincerely sorry for your loss, Raejean." Then I pulled a bead on her behalf and another for Montgomery.

Raejean sniffed again and glanced at the cats. "*They're* not sorry. I can tell by the looks on their ugly faces."

I figured that was Raejean's sorrow speaking. (I'd read about the *stages of grief* in the encyclopedia.) So I ignored the insult.

And then I saw it.

Lying on the sidewalk, pressed up against the building, was something red. I picked it up.

A feather earring. The exact feather earring I'd seen two days ago, dangling from Granny Witch's ear.

I get what I want
And I want what I see
And the girl I marked
Will never stop me.

"Oh, yes I will," I whispered, and handed Raejean the earring. "Give this to the police."

"What is it?" She wrinkled her nose.

"Incriminating evidence," I said, then took off running, the cats panting at my heels.

Chapter 30

I ran all the way to Water Street, not stopping till I reached the dirt yard. I studied the bungalow, wondering where Granny Witch was hiding and if Caleb knew what she'd done with Montgomery. We were in a bad situation—there was no denying it—so I had to be frank with the boys.

"I'm going in, and I need you to follow me, as backup," I said.

Earth hissed.

"This isn't about Raejean and what kind of person she is," I explained. "I don't care if she called you ugly. This is about Montgomery. Can you, in good conscience, live the rest of your life knowing he's in the hands of a *witch*?"

Earth looked down at the sidewalk in shame.

"That's what I thought. Now, all together, run as fast as you can and jump."

We raced across the yard and landed on the front porch with nine satisfying thumps. I knocked on the screen door.

No answer.

I knocked harder. Then I began to pound. I yelled, "Open up, Granny Witch! I know what you did!"

Still no answer.

"Should I?" I asked the cats.

They huddled together, conferring. Then Jupiter stepped forward.

"Meow," he said, which meant, *Go for it*.

So I opened the screen door and placed a hand on the doorknob. I turned.

It opened.

"Shh," I whispered as we crept into the house.

I quickly realized, however, that there was no reason to be quiet. The house was empty. Not only of people, but objects, too. The old couch, the coffee table stacked with ice cream bowls, the TV—all were gone.

"Hello?" I cried. "Is anybody in here?"

Silence.

"Caleb?"

I went to the kitchen. The cupboards were bare,

the refrigerator empty. I found the stairs that led to the second story. Slowly, the cats and I crept up them.

There was a big, empty bedroom with wooden floors. A silver sphere lay in the corner: Granny Witch's crystal ball. I picked it up and raised it to my face. "Show me Montgomery," I said.

The only thing I saw was my own reflection.

There was one other room upstairs, and it, too, was empty save a crooked poster on the wall of a wrestler in tight green pants. I went over to the poster and stared up at the man, whose arms were bent so his muscles popped out.

"Where's Caleb?" I asked him.

The man was silent, but behind me the cats meowed.

They'd discovered something: a row of paper cat heads lined up against the wall, and at the end of the row, a paper football.

I picked up the football and unfolded it.

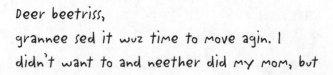

Deer beetriss,
grannee sed it wuz time to move agin. I
didn't want to and neether did my mom, but

grannee sed we had to. That's why I cant
help you fil the eggs. Sorree.

I hope brite babee comes alive and you
turn into a tin man. Tel ur dad hi and that
the muzic in my sole sounds like hundred
dolar bils.

                    Ur frend,
                    the boy in the puffee cote
                    (you kan call me caleb)

The cats wanted me to read the letter out loud,
but it was too hard to speak. The gears in my throat
were flooded. So I folded the note back into a tri-
angle, put it in my pocket, and pulled two beads.
Then I stood there a minute, imagining the bump on
my heart for Caleb.

Finally, we went downstairs. And I saw something
I'd missed before: the bluebird dangled from the light
bulb on the ceiling, still tied up with Granny Witch's
belt.

"Watch this," I told the cats, and jumped as high as
I could, grabbed the cord, and yanked.

The bird snapped free in my hand. I bent low so
the cats could sniff its glassy feathers.

Now what? their curious eyes asked.

"Now we get out of here," I said.

At home, there was a yellow padded envelope lying on the kitchen table. *To Beatrice Corwell*, it said
across the front. Up in the corner were the words
From Dianne.

"She wrote me back!" I yelled. "She finally wrote
me back!" The boys leapt around the room as I tore
open the envelope. Inside was a letter and a small
rock shaped like a horn. I read the letter out loud.

Dear B.,
Greetings from Florida! I'm sorry I took so long to
reply to your postcards. I've just been SO busy since
we moved here.
   I'm happy you found a trilobite! That's really neat.
You can keep it all for yourself because I'm not so
interested in trilobites anymore.
   I've discovered a new fossil: CORAL! There's a girl
in my school who collects it. Her name's Cora. Isn't
that funny? When she found out that I like fossils,
she invited me to join her club: Cora's Coral Club.
She's the president, and I'm the vice president. We
found the enclosed piece of coral just for you! Isn't
it FANTASTIC?

I miss you, Beatrice. I really do. Sometimes I dream that we're making strawberry jam again. And when I wake up, I can taste the sugar on my lips.

Well, I hope you're having fun in Ohio. I like Florida a lot. The ocean is IMMENSE. Maybe someday you'll come visit me. I'll make you an honorary member of the Coral Club!

Love,
D.

I folded the letter in half and put it inside the envelope.

"Meow?" Mercury said.

"It means she's not coming back," I told him.

The boys were crestfallen. And to be honest, I was, too. But you have to put on a brave face when others look up to you.

"It's okay," I said. "We've got other wishes to focus on." I threw my shoulders back, and the boys followed me to my bedroom. I opened my jewelry box, then placed the coral beside Glad's ring, the ring Felix said was worth five thousand dollars.

"Let's look on the bright side," I told the boys. "Now we have two valuable objects in our possession." I smiled reassuringly, and then, when they weren't looking, pulled a bead in my pocket.

* * *

That night, my mom, my dad, and I filled plastic eggs with Tootsie Rolls and Starbursts while the cats batted candy onto the floor. The three of us working together made me imagine another universe, one where my dad didn't disappear, my mom could cut hair in a straight line, and every Christmas we wore matching snowflake sweaters and had our picture taken at Cutie Pie Camera.

My mom snapped a pink egg shut and said, "I don't think two Tootsie Rolls and a Starburst equal a thousand dollars."

"Nobody said they did," my dad said.

"If there's no prize, it's fraud."

"There will be a prize."

"Is it going to fall from the sky, Paul?"

"Maybe." My dad's eyes crinkled. "I don't know particulars. But I do know this: I believe in the power of the Be Bone."

My mom took an *overwhelmed* breath. "I believe in the power of jail."

The cats looked at me. *What do you believe in?* they asked.

I believe in the power of tin, I said, and snapped another egg in half.

✷ ✷ ✷

"A lot happened today, Bright Baby."

It was late, so the room was dark save the fuzzy glimmer from the streetlamps. Bright Baby looked gray and ghostly. The cats' eyes glowed.

"Granny Witch robbed Cutie Pie Camera. She stole Montgomery. Then she took Caleb and his mom, too." I had to stop because my voice was shaking. "The only good part is, I got the bluebird back. It's in my dresser."

I could hear the padding of the cats' feet as they walked atop the comforter.

"Plus, I found out that Dianne of the Flame-Red Hair is staying in Florida. And there's still no prize, Bright Baby, just a bunch of candy. But don't worry. He won't go to jail. I know what to do."

The cats and I left, tiptoed past my mom, who was asleep on the futon, and closed the door to my room.

Plastic eggs filled a row of paper bags along the wall. I picked a purple egg, cracked it open, and emptied the candy onto my bed. Then I went to my dresser and opened the jewelry box. I got out Glad's ring.

Saturn jumped onto the dresser and bit my hand.

"Hey!" I yelled.

He meowed.

"Do you want him to get arrested?" I asked.

Saturn tilted his head as if he didn't care.

"I'm ashamed of all of you," I said, because I could tell all the cats sided with him. "In this family, we help people. We don't just shrug our shoulders and watch them get carted off to jail."

I put the ring in the egg and snapped it closed.

"As a punishment, you may not come with me," I said, and left them there to think about their selfishness.

I slipped past my mom and went down the dark staircase.

The light was on inside GLAD'S. I stood for a moment on the sidewalk. My dad sat on his cot, the golden disc in his palm.

I tapped on the glass.

He glanced up, surprised, and then his eyes crinkled. He opened the door. "What are you still doing up?"

"Can I sleep down here tonight?"

He shrugged. "Sure. Why not?"

I stepped inside.

My dad gestured to the cot. "You can sleep on that luxurious piece of furniture, and I'll take the floor."

"Deal," I said, and stretched out on the cot.

My dad turned off the lights. I heard him lie down beside me. We were quiet in the dark for a while. Then I said, "Dad?"

"Yeah, Bea-Bea?"

"How long do you think it takes someone to become what they're meant to be, once you hold up the Be Bone? Is it instantaneous?"

"I'm not sure."

I nodded, even though he couldn't see me, and then I asked a question that had been bugging me ever since Raejean-Is-Mean had talked about charlatans and chicken bones. "Dad, what if you hold up the Be Bone and nothing happens? What if the person can't hear the music in her soul?"

"I don't think that's a possibility. *Something* is going to happen. I guarantee it."

The shiver of excitement went through me, like a bolt from the blue. "I believe in the power of the Be Bone, Dad. I really do."

"I'm happy to hear it."

"And I believe there's going to be a five-thousand-dollar prize."

"One thousand, you mean," my dad said.

I smiled. "Right."

We were quiet then, and after a minute my dad started snoring. I stared up at a ceiling I couldn't see.

"I believe in the power of the Be Bone," I whispered, the excitement crackling inside me. I pulled a bead.

Less than twenty-four hours till I'd never have to pull a bead again.

Chapter 31

The next morning, I got out my last *Ohio: The Heart of It All!* postcard and gave that obnoxious, steely-eyed cardinal one final stare. Then I wrote:

Dear Caleb,
I miss you. Please come back. I'll wait by the traffic circle. Look for the figure clad in metal.

> Love,
> Your best friend, Beatrice
> (soon to be the Tin Man)

I put the postcard in the mailbox on the street corner and made a wish on the finger that had belonged to Dianne. I didn't have Caleb's address, so all I could do was hope. Hope that the message would get to him somehow. Hope that because the Be Bone was mere hours away from its grand unveiling, there was a magic, stronger than strong, in the air.

My dad hired a crew to set up a stage in the middle of the traffic circle. They brought lights and speakers and a microphone. A banner was draped across the front of the stage that read, COME HEAR THE POWER OF THE BE BONE. There was a table off to the side, where my dad could sell his stickers.

While the crew set up, my dad and I hid the eggs. We placed them all around the traffic circle, and the cats followed along, pointing out good locations with their tails. The sky was gray and dreary.

"I hope it doesn't rain," I said.

"We'll be fine," said my dad.

I didn't say much else, because I was too busy paying attention. Every time I did something—like sneeze, or cough, or trip—I'd think, *That was my last time sneezing (or coughing or tripping) as a sorry-hearted girl. Next time I do it, I'll be a Tin Man.*

When we finished hiding the eggs, my dad said, "I'm going to take a walk now."

"Can I come?" I asked. The cats meowed because they liked going for walks, too.

"Maybe tomorrow, Bea-Bea. I need some alone time—understand?"

I shook my head. "You're always alone, and there is no tomorrow. Tomorrow you leave."

My dad stared at me. His eyes didn't crinkle. Finally, he tugged a lock of my hair. "Your mom really did a number on you with her scissors," he said, then left.

So the boys and I marched over to GLAD'S, where my mom had taped a sign to the door:

Closing early to see Corwell's Cosmic Cats. Join me!

Inside the beauty parlor, Samantha from Panis-Panis sat in a styling chair. My mom was trimming the end of her braid while Elmer, the Doberman pinscher, waited patiently for his bath.

"Hey, Beatrice," Sam said.

"Hi." I looked at my mom's reflection in the mirror. "I didn't know you were coming to see the Be Bone."

"I'm coming to see Corwell's Cosmic Cats," my mom said. "Not Paul's Bizarre Bone."

"I hope I find the prize egg," said Sam.

My mom frowned. "There's no prize."

"Yes, there is," I said.

My mom took a deep breath and went back to trimming the end of Sam's braid.

I stood there, trying to decide if I should tell Sam that this was the last time she'd see me with human skin. Maybe she'd want to take a picture or let Elmer sniff my crooked hair. But I decided not to say anything, because I knew it would make my mom breathe even deeper, since she was an unbeliever, a Be Bone infidel.

Glad, though, was a different story. Bright Baby, too. I had to tell them. The boys and I took our places beside the bed.

"Bright Baby, I'll start with you. I know a lot of this is probably over your head, but today is the day we're going to become what we're meant to be. You'll come to life, and I'll turn into a Tin Man. So don't be scared when I'm all gray and shiny, and if, when I walk, there's a clanking sound. It's still me. I won't hurt you."

Next I focused my mind on the heavenly pool. *Glad, are you listening? I won't have to pull beads pretty soon, and I'll finally stop missing you.* I was quiet for a second, then I added, *Could you finish your message before I become what I'm meant to be? I don't know if Tin Men can read.*

I counted to ten, then opened my eyes.

Bright Baby's eyes were open, too.

"Oh, thank you, Glad!" I cried. "Thank you! Thank you!"

The cats meowed in anticipation.

I reached into the little lace pocket. I unfolded the slip of paper.

Then I froze.

STOP, the paper said, with a period at the end.

"DO NOT TRY TO MAKE THAT WHICH BEATS STOP."

Uranus nudged my hand with his head, wanting me to turn the paper over.

I did. On the back was this: ♡.

Glad wasn't talking about drums. She was talking about my heart. She didn't want me to end the sadness. She didn't want me to make the bumps go flat.

My one and only Glad didn't want me to become a Tin Man.

Never had I felt so furious. Anger boiled inside me like water in a kettle. I caught sight of the valentine, still hanging in the window.

"This is what a beating heart looks like!" I ripped it down.

I saw the encyclopedia set on the bookshelf.

"This is what a beating heart looks like!" I threw the books to the floor.

The cats shrieked and fled the room.

"I'm happy I gave away your ring, Glad! I wish I had another ring of yours so I could give that away, too!"

I turned on my rocket blasters. "This is what a beating heart looks like!"

Apollo 11–style, faster than fast, away I flew.

Chapter 32

I flew to the stage in the middle of the traffic circle. My dad was still on his walk, so I spread out on my back and rubbed the witch mark on my wrist.

The water was probably affecting Glad's thinking. She couldn't see clearly through the heavenly pool. (I'd read about *light refraction* in the encyclopedia.) If she knew what it was like down here without her, she wouldn't have sent that message.

"You can't stop me, Glad. You know that, right?" I said to the gray sky. "If you didn't want me to become a Tin Man, you never should have left."

Lying on an empty stage while fighting with your dead grandma in the middle of the town square is the loneliest feeling in the world. That's the truth and a point-blank fact.

I wished Bright Baby was beside me, and I was blowing bubbles, and she was trying to catch them with her chubby baby hands.

I sat up.

I'd forgotten Bright Baby! I was so angry at Glad's message that I'd left her behind! I had to go get her so we could transform together. The first stop of the Be Bone Tour was less than an hour away.

A shiver of excitement shot through me as I fired up my rocket blasters, then ran.

My mom was waiting outside GLAD'S.

"It's about time, Beatrice! We've got fifteen minutes to get these cats in shape. Come on." She hustled me inside the beauty parlor, where the boys sat in a purple styling chair. My mom grabbed her hair dryer, a comb, and a bottle of spray.

"It's showtime, fellas," she said.

The boys meowed excitedly, and my mom got to work. She dried, combed, and sprayed those cats until their coats were as shiny as a freshly minted penny. Meanwhile, I got out the ironing board and ironed each of their bows. Then my mom and I fastened them around their fluffy necks together.

"They're so handsome," she said.

She was right, of course. "Thank you for helping me."

"Anytime, sweetie." She pulled me close for a hug. "Shall we head over there?"

"You can," I said, "but I have to get something first."

My mom nodded and looked at the cats. "Break some legs."

The boys theatrically swished their tails.

"All right," I said, once my mom had left. "Let's get our girl."

We filed in a line out the door and up the stairs, to Glad's room. And when we got there, I did something I'd never done before. I picked up Bright Baby. I cradled her in my arms.

The cats' mouths fell open, their little white teeth exposed.

"Okay," I said, clutching Bright Baby like the most precious of treasures. "Here we go."

A crowd had gathered in the traffic circle. The cats, Bright Baby, and I weaved through hundreds of people to reach the stage, where my dad stood. He was dressed all in black: button-up shirt, pants, and pointy-toed shoes. The golden disc hung from a chain around his neck. He held a microphone.

His eyes crinkled when he saw me. "I thought you'd gotten cold feet, Bea-Bea."

"Never."

He noticed Bright Baby. "Is the doll part of the act now, too?"

"No. She's here to *become*."

He nodded distractedly. "Look at that crowd."

I looked. I saw Felix, Mrs. Hartley, and Samantha. I saw Nancy, Raejean, and Rabid Rat Boy. I saw a little girl on a man's shoulders holding a sign that read, SHOW ME THE BONE OR I'LL GO HOME! I saw my mom in her *We're GLAD You're Here* shirt.

"Welcome," my dad said into the microphone, "to the first stop on the Be Bone's fifty-state tour."

The crowd cheered.

"Show us the bone!" a man yelled.

"I'll show it to you. Don't worry." My dad's voice echoed through the square. "But first we have eggs to hunt."

"Yippee!" someone cried.

"On the count of three. One . . . two . . . three . . . begin!"

I watched the people fan out, some with baskets, others holding plastic bags or upside-down baseball hats.

"Don't forget: one lucky winner will find a thousand-dollar prize!"

"Five thousand dollars," I murmured, but my dad didn't hear me.

The wind blew, ruffling the cats' fur. The sky was the color of a pigeon.

Mars put his two front paws on my shoe and meowed.

"It's not going to rain," I told him. "Stop worrying."

But the smell of rain whipped through the air.

After thirty minutes had passed, my dad said into the microphone, "Please return to the stage."

Once the people had reassembled, their baskets and bags and ball caps brimming with eggs, he said, "Now open your finds, and let's congratulate the winner!"

I held Bright Baby close to my chest and watched as they cracked their eggs in half. I hoped somebody good would find the ring, somebody who loved beautiful things. I hoped I'd be able to smile when whoever it was placed it on their finger.

"Only Tootsie Rolls," a man yelled.

"Just Starbursts," cried another.

But then a third voice drifted faintly from the crowd: "I found it! I found it!"

The people parted.

And there stood Raejean in a pink polo dress, triumphantly holding Glad's ring in the air.

Chapter 33

"Come up here, and let's see what you've got," my dad said.

Raejean climbed the stage stairs, then handed him the ring. My dad whistled into the microphone.

"Well, look at that."

I couldn't tell if he recognized the ring, if he knew what I'd done. My mom did, though. She stood in the front row and closed her eyes. Beside her, Felix shook his head. The cats, up onstage beside me, arched their backs and hissed.

I bit the inside of my cheeks and blinked back tears. To see your most valuable possession in the hands of your nemesis is like a giant boot on your chest.

"Looks like we have a winner," my dad said. "What's your name, sweetheart?"

"Raejean," Raejean said, curtsying in a super-fake way.

The people cheered. Mrs. Hartley yelled, "That's my student up there!" Raejean retook her place in the crowd.

"Now," my dad said, "we have a very special performance. All the way from the GLAD'S building, please welcome the world premiere of Corwell's Cosmic Cats!"

He pointed at me, then stepped to the side of the stage.

I looked at the cats, huddled dejectedly at my feet. "The show must go on," I told them. Then I squeezed Bright Baby to my chest. "This one's for you," I whispered before handing her to my dad.

I arranged the cats in two straight lines, then went to the front of the stage, where a gust of wind lifted my hair.

"The fish swims this way." They stepped to the right. "The fish swims that way." They stepped to the left. "The fish swims far." A step back. "The fish swims near." A step forward. "A worm's on the hook!" They swished their tails and meowed.

I turned to face the audience.

The crowd went wild.

"Woo!" they yelled. "More! More!"

It was the most wonderful feeling in the world, all that goodwill. My heart was fuller than full—and for the first time, I wondered if maybe Glad was right. Maybe a person shouldn't try to make that which beats stop. But then I remembered that a heart wasn't all my-cats-can-dance happiness. Tears and ripping down valentines—those were what a beating heart looked like, too.

My dad handed me Bright Baby as the crowd continued to clap.

"How about those cats?" he said.

The boys and I stepped offstage while Felix stuck two thumbs in the air and my mom yelled, "Beatrice Corwell rules!"

Which was kind of embarrassing, but also good.

"All right, folks. Now it's time to get down to business," said my dad.

"Looks like rain," someone in the audience called out.

My dad tilted his face to the sky. The pigeon gray had darkened; the clouds were foreboding.

"You think a little rain is going to stop us?" my dad asked, opening the golden disc around his neck. He removed the bone and held it high over his head. "Behold the Be Bone!" he cried.

Under the dark sky, the bone glowed brighter than bright.

"Aaah," the crowd said.

Thunder boomed.

"I was a DJ, but I was playing the wrong tunes." My dad walked back and forth across the stage. "This bone taught me to hear!"

"I wanna hear!" a woman screamed.

"You will. You *all* will," my dad said. Then he told the story of being drunk on the highway and waking up to find the Be Bone in his hand. "I heard a new song and became a different person that day. Now it's your turn to hear and become. Who's first?"

The traffic circle was silent as the rain began to fall. No one stepped forward or raised a hand.

So I said, "I am," and returned to the center of the stage.

"You, Bea-Bea?" my dad said, surprised.

I nodded and wondered if he'd still call me Bea-Bea when I was made of tin.

The wind howled, and Glad's voice drifted from far away: *Do not try to make that which beats stop.*

No, Glad, I thought. *It's too late now!*

My dad raised the Be Bone high above my head. It was pouring, and the rain was icy cold.

"Listen to the song inside you!" my dad cried over the storm. "Become what you're meant to be! Behold the power of the Be Bone!"

I raised Bright Baby up to the rolling sky. "Oh, pretty please," I whispered. "Let us become together."

There was a cracking sound, and a flash of light.

Then silence, followed by a mournful wail.

"The siren," somebody yelled.

"Tornado!" cried another.

And that's when I saw the great twisting funnel cloud in the sky.

Chapter 34

The rain fell, the tornado spun, and the crowd screamed.

"Get to GLAD'S," my dad yelled into the microphone. "Seek shelter immediately!"

"Run, boys!" I told the cats. "Run!"

And run we did: me, the cats, my dad, and a couple hundred others. We ran across the circle, then the street, then jumped the curb, and ran down the sidewalk, to where Felix stood outside GLAD'S, holding open the door.

"In here!" he cried, his bald head glistening. "Right in here!"

There was no way we could all fit inside, but somehow we did. People sat in the styling chairs and in the sinks, and the rest of us crammed together, wet and windblown, without an inch to spare.

The wind howled, and through the front windows, we could see a sky so dark it was nearly black. Then it sounded like a train, and the building shook. People cried and screamed. I held Bright Baby tighter than tight against my chest.

Then, suddenly, it stopped. The world was still. The tornado had passed.

"It's over," somebody said.

"Oh, thank you, God!" cried another.

The GLAD'S door opened. People spilled like water onto the sidewalk. The cats and I were swept along in the current.

Outside, the sun shone brightly, as if the storm had never happened, but debris was everywhere. An awning lay mangled in the street; broken windows lined the square; tree branches were strewn all over the sidewalks. The mailbox that held Caleb's postcard was tipped on its side, and my dad's stage was upside down. His stickers had scattered and were plastered on buildings and traffic signs, like graffiti. GLAD'S, though, was unharmed. It stood tall and proud, its big purple letters a victory sign.

My dad appeared. "Wow," he said. "That was something, huh?"

"It was a tornado," I told him, "and your stickers are stuck all over town."

He laughed, and his eyes crinkled. "The Be Bone's revenge." Then he said, "There are forty-nine more stops on the tour."

"I know how many states there are. I've read a twenty-six-volume encyclopedia set."

"That's quite the achievement, Bea-Bea. It really is." He paused. "I'm going to get in my truck now."

That was his way of saying goodbye. He never said the actual word. He just sort of left.

I looked at his dark goatee, his crinkly eyes. I wanted to hug him, but if I hugged him, it would mean I one hundred percent knew he was leaving. And I didn't want to know that yet. So I didn't hug him. I just said, "See you, Dad."

"That's right, Bea-Bea. See you." He tugged my hair. Then he walked away.

I stared at the back of him, knowing I wouldn't see the front for two years. I'd be twelve when my dad came back, almost thirteen. I might have my ears pierced then. I might have another cat. Two years is a long time.

And it was only then, thinking about my future self, that I realized I still was who I'd always been: a lonely, crooked-haired girl. I hadn't been transformed into a Tin Man. And Bright Baby was no sister, just an old porcelain doll in a pretty lace dress.

The truth of this was a tower of bricks upon my head.

I cradled her in my arms. "Oh, Bright Baby, nothing went according to plan." I reached for a bead in my pocket, but the cord was gone. It must have fallen out when I ran from the tornado.

Anger flamed up inside me, big as a bonfire. I looked around, eyes burning, and the first thing I saw was a sticker—*Tired of the dead zone? Then listen to the Be Bone*—plastered on a store window.

I ripped it off.

Then I saw one on the seat of a bench. I ripped that off, too.

The more I looked, the more stickers I saw, stuck on lampposts and planters and trash cans. I ripped them all off. I was a runaway rocket, on fire and off course, ripping sticker after sticker as the cats meowed at my heels.

Then I was out of gas.

I slumped down onto a lamppost that had been

torn from the sidewalk. And as soon as I did, the tears fell. This time, no matter how tightly I squeezed my eyes, I couldn't stop them.

That's how my mom found me: sobbing, tears on my arms and legs, cats licking tears from my shins.

"Beatrice!" she yelled. "Finally! I didn't know where you were!" And then she saw my face. "Oh, sweetie. What happened?"

"Nothing," I said. "Everything. He's gone. But my heart's still here."

"Paul always leaves," my mom said, sitting beside me, "but he'll come back."

"Not till I'm almost thirteen. That's a long time."

"That is a long time," she said.

There were sirens in the distance. We listened to them wail. Then my mom put her arm around me.

"I'm happy your heart's still here, by the way."

I stared at the sidewalk. "I wanted to be a Tin Man."

"I like you how you are," my mom said.

Snot ran from my nose. I wiped it with the back of my hand. My eyes felt puffy, and I knew my face was a mottled red. "This is what a beating heart looks like," I said. "Not too pretty, huh?"

"No, not *pretty*. It's the most *beautiful* thing there is."

"Don't sell GLAD'S," I whispered.

My mom's arm tightened around my shoulder.

"Selling GLAD'S is the last thing I want to do. But sometimes, Beatrice, the last thing must be done."

I closed my eyes and held Bright Baby to my chest. "That's how it was with Glad's ring. Giving it to Rae-jean was the last thing I wanted to do."

My mom sighed. "I know."

We were quiet, and then she said, "Let's go home."

"I can't. My heart— It's used up all the strength I possessed." That was the truth and a point-blank fact. I was so tired, I couldn't stand.

Then my *overwhelmed* mom did something kind of amazing. Somehow, she summoned the strength of a lion and picked me up, like I was her Bright Baby, like I was the most important thing in the world.

And she carried me like that, in her arms, down the sidewalk, all eight of the boys making straight our path.

Chapter 35

I slept for a long time: the rest of the day, all through the night, and late the next morning. When I finally woke up, Bright Baby was tucked beside me, and the cats were curled, eight furry humps, on the bed.

My mom was in the room, wearing her *We're GLAD You're Here* shirt. Felix stood beside her, along with Samantha and Nancy.

"We didn't mean to wake you," my mom said, "but Felix has something he wants to tell you."

"Actually, I have something I want to *give* you. Hold out your hand." Felix reached into his pocket, then dropped something into my palm.

It was Glad's flower ring.

The cats were shocked.

"How did you get it?" I asked.

"I bought it from Raejean. Paid one thousand dollars cash—the deal of the century, since, as you know, the ring has been appraised at five times that."

I slipped the ring onto my finger, where it sparkled in the late-morning light.

"What do you say, Beatrice?" my mom asked.

I was supposed to say thank you, of course, but different words came out: "I'm the one who took your bluebird. I was mad at you for making the FOR SALE sign, so I stole it."

Felix was silent.

"I got it back, though. It's in the top drawer of my dresser. Please get it."

He opened the drawer and got out the bluebird. The instant he held it, his face shone pure, freshly squeezed happiness. "Thank you, Miss Corwell."

"The pleasure is mine, Mr. Farmer."

Then my mom asked something weird. "What did you put in Bright Baby's pocket?"

"Nothing," I said.

Felix laughed. "That's the lumpiest nothing I've ever seen."

He was right. There was a big lump in the middle of her dress.

Neptune meowed, and Mercury nudged my hand with his head.

"Hold on. Give me a second." I slipped my fingers into the lace. When I pulled them out, I held a tiny plastic egg.

"How did that get in there?" my mom asked.

"Open it," said Felix.

I twisted the egg. A silver heart fell onto the bed.

"Will you look at that?" said Nancy.

Felix picked it up. "It's got a ring at the top. I think it's to be worn on a necklace." He handed me the heart.

I studied it. "Where did it come from?" But before anyone could answer, I realized what I held: the heart of a Tin Man.

"Oh," I said, then closed my eyes and focused on the heavenly pool.

Glad was no longer floating. She sat cross-legged on the pool's edge, fingertips pressed together.

Who's it for? I asked. Even though I knew, I wanted to hear her say it.

Glad smiled. Her hair was the color of gold, and her face glowed. *You, my dear Beatrice. Always and forever you.*

"Beatrice," said my mom. "There's something else." She looked at Nancy.

"Your cats were a sensation," the insurance agent said. "Everybody's talking about them."

"And we mean *everybody*," Sam jumped in. "And not just what they *did*, but how they *looked*."

"That fur!" Nancy cried. "So clean and fluffy!"

"That's my mom's doing," I told them. "She's the boys' stylist."

"We know!" Sam said, exchanging a smile with Nancy. "And it's not just cats—she's done wonders for Elmer and Sprinkles, too."

Nancy nodded. "That's what gave us the idea."

"What if," Sam continued, "instead of a place where *people* got haircuts, GLAD'S was a place where *animals* got styled?"

I looked at my mom.

"I want to turn GLAD'S into a pet-grooming store," she said.

"You mean, you wouldn't have to sell it?" I asked.

"That's right." She smiled. "And in addition to pet *grooming*, I thought there could be pet *training* as well. What do you say, Felix?"

Felix turned to me. "What do *you* think, Beatrice? Should we teach everyone's cats how to dance?"

"You'd want me to help you?" I asked.

He nodded. "How could I not include the town's expert on feline care?"

Felix thought I was an expert! GLAD'S wasn't going to be sold! My mom was finally going to do something she was good at! Joy flooded my heart, wave after wave, so much I didn't think I could stand it.

But I did.

I watched Felix reach for my mom's hand. "Marta, there's nothing I'd rather do than start this business together."

And do you know what? My mom didn't take an *overwhelmed* breath. Instead, she said, "The feeling is mutual," and then she laughed. Holding Felix's hand, she laughed and laughed.

My whole entire life, I'd never seen her look so happy. That's the truth and a point-blank fact.

So that's how I knew, even before they announced it, that my mom and Felix would start bowling again. Which is another way of saying, sometime, in the not-too-distant future, the fantastic Farmer would become my dad.

Chapter 36

A rainbow appeared that afternoon. I'd read about *rainbows* in the encyclopedia, so I knew they were watery reflections of light. But this one appeared out of nowhere, without any rain, and it stretched across the sky, so big and impossibly bright. It was the kind of phenomenon that made you suspect something significant was about to happen. So I went outside to make sure I was present when it did.

The downtown was still a mess, with tree limbs stacked on the sidewalk and businesses with boarded windows. But the rainbow made everything look better, bolder, full of color. The cats and I were staring up at it when I heard a muffled cry.

The boys looked at me.

The cry was feline, which meant we were about to add a new member to our family. Neptune meowed in consternation. I'd told him he was the last planet, so his dismay was justified.

"Don't worry. You're still the final planet. The new guy can be Moon," I said.

We traced the cries to the waterspout; then I dropped to my stomach and peered inside. I couldn't see anything, but I heard little puffs of breath.

"I'm going to save you," I told the kitten.

"Who you talkin' to?" a voice asked.

The voice, unfortunately, did not belong to the cat.

I was too tired to count to twenty, so I decided to ignore the voice instead. I reached my arm into the waterspout.

"Oh, I know," the voice said. "There's somethin' you want in there."

The voice was smart.

I felt soft, fluffy fur.

"And since you're talkin' to it, it must be a critter of some sort."

The voice was *very* smart.

A warm, wet tongue licked my hand.

"I'm guessin' it's a cat in there."

The voice was practically a genius.

I wrapped my hand around the soft little body and pulled.

"That's no cat!" the voice cried. "That's a dog!"

The voice was right.

There I sat on the sidewalk, holding Montgomery in my hand. His orange fur was dirty, but his eyes were alert, and his tongue was as pink and sticking out as ever.

The cats sniffed him, one by one.

"Now, how'd he get in there?" the voice asked, and then a body crouched beside me and a hand petted the top of Montgomery's head.

It was Caleb! He had on new bright red sneakers and a blue-checkered shirt in place of his puffy coat.

"Caleb!" I cried. "What are you doing here?"

"You're the one who asked me to come back." He reached into his shirt pocket and pulled out the postcard with the steely-eyed cardinal.

The cats were as surprised as I was.

"How'd you get it?" I asked, cradling Montgomery in my lap. "I didn't know your address."

Caleb smiled. "Twister brought it."

"And what about Granny Witch? I thought she kidnapped you."

"Nah. She just made me and my mom move again,

but then somethin' funny happened after we left. My mom started thinkin' about the promotion she got and how good she was at makin' garage doors, and she decided she didn't want to keep on followin' Granny around anymore. So we came back."

"And you're going to stay?"

"Yep."

I looked at the cats. "Did you hear that, boys?"

The cats let out excited cries, then went wild, leaping like jackrabbits through the air.

Caleb laughed. "They kinda look like leprechauns," he said, which, of course, they did *not*, but I didn't care.

"Oh, Caleb, I *wished* you'd come back."

"I guess your wish came true, Beatrice." Caleb paused, then asked, "But what about the Tin Man?"

I touched the pendant hanging from my neck. "The only metal thing I have is this." I held up the heart so he could see it.

Caleb leaned in so close that I could count his freckles. "Pretty cool. But are you sad?"

"No, because really good things are happening now. My mom isn't going to sell GLAD'S. She's going to open a pet-grooming store, and Felix and I are going to train cats."

"Well, that's just how it goes," Caleb said. "A whole

bunch of bad stuff happens all in a row, and you think it'll never get better, but then, one day when you're least expectin' it, it does."

"That's exactly right!"

Caleb proudly patted his porcupine quills. "I'm supersmart."

"There's just one thing."

"Bright Baby?"

I nodded.

Caleb bit his lip. "I knew that was gonna be a hard one."

"She was my biggest, tip-top secret wish."

Caleb tugged his earlobe. "Well, a whole bunch of your wishes came true, right? So I think you should focus on that. And maybe it's good if you don't get everything you want, because if you did, you'd turn into a spoiled brat."

"You mean like Raejean?" I asked.

"Yep."

In my lap, Montgomery yipped, then began licking my wrist.

"He looks like he's eatin' a lollipop!" Caleb cried.

"What are you doing, silly?" I asked the puppy, but Montgomery just kept licking, his tiny tongue warm and wet.

Neptune nudged my hand with his head.

"What is it?" I asked, but before he could tell me, I saw. The witch mark was gone! Montgomery had licked it away! "Look, Caleb!" I flashed my bare wrist. "The spell is broken!"

"Oh, man!"

Montgomery hopped from my lap and ran in circles, and then the cats joined in. Caleb and I jumped and high-fived in the air.

"I can't believe it's gone!"

Caleb raised his fist to the sky. "Never underestimate the power of Pomeranians!"

I scooped up Montgomery and snuggled him against my chest. Then I turned to Caleb. "Do you think we should return this puppy to its rightful owner?"

"If that means Raejean, then, no," Caleb said.

I laughed and looked at Montgomery's dirty fur. "Actually, maybe we should keep him a *little* longer, so my mom can wash him. Montgomery, do you want to be the new and improved GLAD'S first customer?"

Montgomery yipped.

"Let me hold him," Caleb said.

So I handed the puppy over, and Caleb and I walked toward GLAD'S, the boys trailing single file behind us. And I thought, *What if Raejean's mom took a picture of us, walking side by side with Montgomery and the cats?* I bet we'd look so happy. I bet anyone who saw us would think, *Look at those two. They must be best friends. I wish I had a friend like that.*

I smiled at Caleb, and he smiled back.

And my heart, my beautiful, beating heart, leapt inside my chest.

Acknowledgments

I'm so grateful to have this book published. An enormous thank-you to everyone who aided in its completion.

Caroline Abbey, my editor at Random House Children's Books, makes my writing better. She sees what I somehow missed and helps bring the important into focus.

Kerry Sparks, my literary agent at Levine Greenberg Rostan, always has time for *everything*. I'm lucky to have her on my team.

The cats of my childhood—Sunshine, Misty, Calvin, Ozzie, Wo, Candy, and Lolla (who was found in a waterspout)—provided years of companionship and, later, much inspiration.

My mom dutifully cared for all the aforementioned

felines—even the ones I begged for and promised to look after myself. Thank you, Mom, for making sure we were all fed.

My four children are ever eager to help with brainstorming and giving feedback. What a joy it is to share my work with them.

And to my husband, who washes the dishes, makes sure all the teeth get brushed, and hunts down missing pajamas so I can have space to write: Mike, your devotion is unparalleled. That's the truth and a point-blank fact.